••••••••••••••••••••••••••••

MEG
AND THE
MYSTERY IN
WILLIAMSBURG

••••••••••••••••••••••••••••

ABOUT THIS BOOK

A hidden chimney door . . . Miss Mariah's secret . . .
the disappearance of Paris, Miss Mariah's childhood
doll . . . muddy footprints on the back stairs . . . the
missing valuable toys . . . the clues in the old diary
. . . these were some of the things that puzzled Meg
when she went to Williamsburg with her Uncle Hal
and her best friend, Kerry Carmody.

Working with Kerry as a junior hostess at the toy
show, Meg soon found that her talent for discovering
things was leading them into danger. What were the
suspicious strangers after? Why were she and Kerry
locked in the old jail? And who chased them in the
garden? These were only a few of the questions Meg
needed to answer.

As the pieces of the puzzle fell into place, Meg solved
the mystery of the secret room and finally pieced
together the remaining clues in MYSTERY IN
WILLIAMSBURG.

MYSTERY IN WILLIAMSBURG

by Holly Beth Walker

illustrated by Cliff Schule
cover illustration by Olindo Giacomini

GOLDEN PRESS
Western Publishing Company, Inc.
Racine, Wisconsin

CONTENTS

1

THE CHIMNEY DOOR

"Dandelions," Meg Duncan said aloud, although she was alone. "A few yellow dandelions. . . ."

She stepped back from her easel and looked at the sketch she had just made of the meadows behind the house. Green and sweet with new spring grass and polka-dotted with big white daisies, the rolling countryside made a beautiful picture. Meg had hurried home from school to sketch it.

It was a lovely April afternoon. The sun was so warm that the kitchen windows and door were wide open. Meg could hear Mrs. Wilson, the housekeeper, at her work.

Meg's mother was dead, and Mrs. Wilson took care of the Duncan house for Meg and her father. Mr. Wilson, her husband, did the yard work and odd jobs. Meg's father had an important government job. Since he was away from home so much,

Meg spent a lot of time with the Wilsons.

Meg picked out a yellow pastel stick for the dandelions in her sketch. *I'll call it "Springtime in Hidden Springs, Virginia,"* she thought. *When Daddy comes home from his trip, he can see how pretty our meadows looked this year.*

Inside the house, a cat howled in anger. A bundle of cream and brown fur came streaking out the kitchen door, with Mrs. Wilson right behind it.

"Oh, my, oh, my, Thunder! I am sorry," she said, "but you are always under my feet!"

"Thunder!" Meg scolded gently. "Were you in Mrs. Wilson's way again? Shame on you."

The big Siamese cat's long tail stopped lashing the air, but he continued to glare at the housekeeper. His eyes, blue and slanty, said very plainly, "I'm Meg's cat. I take my orders from her—and don't you forget that, Mrs. Wilson."

Disdainfully, Thunder turned his back and jumped up onto Meg's patio chair. He looked so haughty and regal that Meg burst out laughing. Even Mrs. Wilson had to smile.

"Margaret Ashley Duncan," she said, "that cat belongs in the movies. He's a born actor."

Tilting her head, Mrs. Wilson examined Meg's sketch. "That's real pretty," she said.

Meg stood off and viewed her work again. "It still needs something," she said slowly. "I wish Uncle

12

Hal were here to help me.''

Mrs. Wilson clapped her hands in dismay. ''Oh, my, oh, my,'' she cried. ''That cat made me forget why I was coming out here. Your Uncle Hal is here to see you.''

Meg was across the patio and into the house before Mrs. Wilson had finished speaking.

Next to her father, Meg loved Hal Ashley better than anyone else in the world. Meg's mother and Uncle Hal had been brother and sister. Meg was very much like her uncle, and they always had fun together. Uncle Hal never just ''did things''; he had ''adventures.'' Meg was sure he carried excitement around in his pockets the way other people carry nickels and dimes.

Uncle Hal drove a beautiful antique Duesenberg roadster and flew his own airplane. He had an apartment in Washington, D.C., and a hideaway cabin in Maine. Even his job, with a Washington museum, was different and exciting.

Meg ran through the kitchen and down the long hallway to the library. Uncle Hal was sitting on the sofa, frowning over a long, typed report he held in his hand. Meg knew at once it was important. Her uncle was so interested in his reading that he didn't even see Meg standing in the doorway.

''Uncle Hal''—Meg spoke softly—''if you're busy. . . .''

13

Hal Ashley looked up at once. "Maggie-me-love," he laughed. "Come on in. Business can wait." Hastily Meg's handsome young uncle pushed the report into his briefcase and snapped the lock. Moving over, he made room for Meg on the sofa.

"You know, you look more like your mother every day, Meg," he said. "The same brown eyes, same smile, same dark hair. Only—" he gave Meg's braid a tug—"only my sister didn't have pigtails."

"Oh, Uncle Hal! Don't be such a tease," Meg said as she flipped her long braids off her shoulders impatiently.

Her uncle laughed and leaned back against the cushions. "Maggie-me-love," he said, "do you remember Lucy Cameron?"

"Of course," Meg answered quickly. "Lucy was my mother's best friend. They were always together —the way Kerry Carmody and I are."

Meg knew all about her mother's childhood friend. Lucy Cameron lived in Williamsburg. Her work with the restoration program there was well known. The Cameron family's old scrapbooks, records, and writings had been invaluable in restoring the streets and buildings of Williamsburg to look as they did in Colonial days.

Uncle Hal saw Lucy often. They were in similar lines of work, and both had a definite talent for discovering things.

14

"Does Lucy still live in the little house where my mother used to go for vacations?" Meg asked.

Uncle Hal nodded. "She does," he said, smiling. "And Lucy's been working for months collecting old-fashioned toys for a toy exhibition. She's had everyone in town searching attics and finding things for her. Even Miss Mariah Collins has agreed to lend Lucy some Colonial clothes."

"Miss Mariah Collins . . . what a pretty, old-fashioned name," Meg said.

"Miss Mariah is an old-fashioned lady," her uncle continued. "She is old and wealthy—and a bit odd. I don't know Miss Mariah too well, but she's a good friend of Lucy's. She was very fond of your mother, too, Meg. She lives in a beautiful big plantation house that her great-great-grandfather built, and—" Uncle Hal paused—"and it seems to me I remember that there's some kind of a mystery about Miss Mariah and that old house. Something about a locked room on the top floor—and an old doll that she carries around."

"Really?" Meg broke in. She loved mysteries. "Go on!"

Uncle Hal gave her a quick hug. "You'll get to see it all for yourself, Maggie," he said. "How would you like to go to Williamsburg with me next week?"

Meg's eyes sparkled. "You mean on vacation?" she asked.

"Well . . . not exactly, Meg," he answered thoughtfully. "I'll be quite busy—with some business."

"I know," Meg said, nodding wisely. "Museum business," she said. "And I'm not supposed to ask questions about it."

"Right!" Hal laughed. "You kids are going to be pretty busy, too. Lucy wants you and Kerry Carmody to help her with the toy show as junior hostesses."

Meg's brown eyes widened with excitement. "I'll call Kerry right this minute!" she cried.

Kerry answered the phone on the first ring. "Hello," she shouted.

The noise and confusion of the Carmody house exploded in Meg's ear and made her giggle. Kerry had five brothers and a little sister, and her home was always noisy. Meg could hear a small Carmody loudly demanding a "dink of water."

"Kerry," Meg said, "want to go to Williamsburg?"

Kerry didn't need to be coaxed. "When do we leave?" she shouted over the noise. "I'm ready!"

Uncle Hal laughed as he took the phone from Meg. "No horses down there, Kerry," he reminded her. "But if your mother says you can go, start packing. We leave tomorrow, as soon as school closes for vacation."

At five o'clock the next afternoon, Uncle Hal drove slowly down the wide Duke of Gloucester

16

Street, under an arch of tree branches. Williamsburg looked almost sleepy in the warm April twilight. Rain clouds hid the sun, leaving shadows on the red brick sidewalks.

Down the street, a horse and carriage clip-clopped along. The driver raised his tricornered hat and bowed as he rode past the Duesenberg roadster.

Meg and Kerry loved the old-fashioned setting. They were almost sorry when Hal Ashley left the main road and turned down Lucy's quiet street.

"That rain cloud's getting lower," he said. "Lucy won't be home from work yet, but we can go right in. The front door is always open."

A few minutes later, they pulled up in front of the old Cameron home. Twin rows of old boxwoods bordered the narrow pathway that led up to the front door. The house was painted white, with shiny black shutters at every window, and at one side there was a giant red brick chimney, almost as wide as the house itself.

It was beginning to rain as they stepped onto the sidewalk. Uncle Hal stopped to put up the top of his roadster and lift out his briefcase. Meg and Kerry raced for the front door. Seconds later, Hal joined them. He pushed against the door, but it didn't open.

"Guess it's locked, after all," Meg said.

"It can't be," Uncle Hal insisted. "Lucy never

17

locks this door. Uh-oh," he broke off, "I know why. The front door sticks in damp weather."

"How about the back door, Mr. Ashley?" Kerry suggested.

Uncle Hal shook his head. "No use, Kerry. Lucy always keeps the back door locked."

Meg giggled. "If we were Santa Claus, we could go down the chimney," she said. "It's big enough."

"That's it!" Uncle Hal snapped his fingers, suddenly remembering something. "The chimney door! Lucy always uses the chimney door when it rains."

Meg and Kerry exchanged glances.

"What's a chimney door, Uncle Hal?" Meg asked quickly.

Hal laughed at them. "Sounds mysterious, doesn't it, Maggie?" he said. "You can't see it from the street. You have to go all the way around back. Come on."

The rain was coming down hard now. Meg and Kerry hurried up the side path and around past the giant brick chimney after Uncle Hal.

Cut into the house, close beside the back end of the big chimney, the narrow "chimney door" was almost hidden. It had been made so carefully that it hardly showed. There was no sign of a doorknob.

Uncle Hal ran his fingers along the side of the door, hunting for a tiny hidden spring. There was a soft *click,* and the door swung outward.

18

"Okay, kids," he said. "Let's get out of this downpour."

The room was dark and musty-smelling. There were no windows, and Meg could tell there was no floor. She could feel the hard-packed dirt under her feet.

"It's kind of spooky in here, Uncle Hal," Meg said.

Kerry inched her fingers along a wall. "I feel bricks," she said. "Are we right inside the chimney, Mr. Ashley?"

Uncle Hal laughed. "Not quite, Kerry," he answered. "The door was beside the chimney, not in it. That's the side of the chimney you're touching. We're in Lucy's old woodshed."

A tiny beam of light from Hal Ashley's pencil flashlight crawled slowly around the room. It barely showed the dark corners.

"The shed is empty now, of course," Hal told them. "But when the Cameron house was heated by fireplaces, this place was full of wood."

Meg's eyes were getting used to the darkness. She could make out the outline of a door on one wall.

At that moment the door was flung open, and Lucy Cameron stood silhouetted in the opening. "Who's in there?" she demanded. "Whoever you are, come out of my woodshed!"

"You bet we will." Hal Ashley laughed as he

walked into the living room. Meg and Kerry followed him.

"Meg—and Kerry—and Hal Ashley!" Lucy exclaimed. "Why in the world were you in the woodshed?"

Hal put his briefcase on a chair. "Why in the world don't you get your front door fixed so a person can come in out of the rain?" he asked good-naturedly.

Lucy put on a haughty face. "It's an old family tradition, Mr. Ashley," she said primly. "The Cameron front door is *supposed* to stick when it rains."

Lucy burst out laughing then and hugged Meg and Kerry fondly. "I'm so glad you came for the toy show," she said. "We need you."

Hal sniffed the air. "Mmm," he said, "something smells nice."

Lucy gave him a sly look from the corner of her eye. "It could be my new perfume," she said. "But I rather think you mean the food. Dinner is almost ready."

Ten minutes later they were at the dinner table, eating roast chicken and hot honey biscuits. While they ate, Lucy told them about the toy show.

The exhibition was to be held in the Child's Room at Brush-Everard House, one of the oldest houses in Williamsburg.

"The house once belonged to Mr. William Dering,

the Williamsburg dancing master. He was an artist,
too. Some of his paintings are hanging in the living
room there,'' Lucy explained.

She went on talking about the show. All the toys
had been lent to her by old Williamsburg families.
They had searched their attics and cellars, finding
old toys that had been forgotten for many years.
And Miss Mariah Collins had sent over some of her
own Colonial costumes for the junior hostesses.

Meg recognized the name. "Uncle Hal told us
about Miss Mariah," she said. "She sounds kind of
mysterious."

"She isn't really," Lucy said. "She's a good friend
of mine, and she was very fond of your mother, Meg.
We were the only little girls in town who were ever
invited out to River House. That's the name of Miss
Mariah's old plantation house, out on the old river
road. When her family built it, about three hundred
years ago, the land and fields ran right down to the
river. But that's all changed now. Most of the land
has been cut up for new roads and buildings. Only
the old plantation house is left. Everybody calls it the
old Collins mansion, except Miss Mariah and me.
We still say River House.

"Miss Mariah is old, and she has odd little ways
about her," Lucy went on. "She often carries an old-
fashioned doll under her arm. And townspeople say
she has one room on the top floor of her house that

21

she has kept locked for over forty years.''

"Wow!'' Kerry exclaimed.

"But why?'' Meg asked quickly.

Lucy didn't know why. "Nobody in Williamsburg knows why,'' she said. "But they say''—Lucy's voice was very serious now—"that every afternoon, between two and three o'clock, Miss Mariah goes upstairs, unlocks the door, and goes into that room. And then she closes and locks the door behind her.''

Meg's and Kerry's eyes were as round as saucers.

Lucy's soft laughter broke the spell. "Anyway,'' she said, "maybe we'll find out something tomorrow. Miss Mariah wants to see you girls dressed in your Colonial costumes. She asked me to bring you out to River House tomorrow—about two-thirty in the afternoon.''

2
MISS MARIAH'S SECRET

Meg stood in front of the mirror, winding the wide sash around her waist. The sash was pink and matched the underskirt beneath the cream-colored silk dress. With her long braids tied with pink bows and her black ballet slippers peeking out from beneath her skirt, Meg looked exactly like a little girl from Colonial days.

Tomboy Kerry made a darling boy in black knee breeches, white shirt, and high white stockings. Her shiny blond hair was brushed into a smooth pageboy.

"Oh, Kerry," Meg said the minute she saw her friend, "I have to sketch you in that outfit so I can show Daddy."

"Okay," Kerry agreed. "Maybe when we get back from Miss Mariah's. Lucy is waiting for us now. Come on."

Downstairs, Uncle Hal was using the dining room

table for his office. Papers and notebooks were spread around him in disorder. Meg thought her uncle looked worried. She had seen her father look the same way when he was working on something special.

"Don't go in now," she whispered to Kerry. "He's too busy."

Hal Ashley heard her and looked up from his work. "Oh, hi, kids. I like your outfits. Miss Mariah should be pleased. I wish I were going along with you, instead of going off on business."

He started to gather up his papers. Meg hurried over to the table to help him. "Never mind, Maggie," Hal said, rather sharply. "I'll do it."

He crammed the papers into his briefcase and gave Meg a quick hug. " 'Bye, Maggie," he said. "Have fun. I'll see you tonight."

Kerry had gone outside to find Lucy. Meg decided to straighten up the dining room. As she moved Uncle Hal's chair, she saw a piece of paper on the seat. It was a newspaper clipping—a picture of a young man.

He was a neat-looking person. His clothes looked expensive. His hair was combed straight back from his face, and he was almost smiling. But there wasn't a hint of a smile in his eyes. They seemed to stare out at Meg, and they gave her an uncomfortable feeling.

This must belong to Uncle Hal, she decided. *I'll put it in his room.*

Running upstairs, Meg tucked the clipping under the frame of Uncle Hal's mirror. Then she hurried out to Lucy's station wagon.

Miss Mariah Collins's house was as stately as a mansion and as quiet as a church. Meg felt like whispering and walking on tiptoe as she and Kerry followed Lucy across the wide, dim hallway. The old housekeeper had let them in and directed them to the parlor.

Lucy stopped at the open door. "Afternoon, Miss Mariah," she called.

Small and dainty, dressed in a soft gray that matched her hair, Miss Mariah Collins sat on the old-fashioned sofa. Beside her, as prim and proper as the lady herself, sat a lovely old doll.

"Come in, Lucy," Miss Mariah said. She had the slow, gentle southern slur in her words, and she didn't sound nearly as old as she looked.

Lucy led the way into the room. "Here we are," she said. "This is—"

With a wave of her hand, Mariah stopped the introduction. "I know who these two children are, Lucy," she said with a faint smile. "The 'boy' must be Kerry, and the girl is Meg. I would know Margaret Ashley Duncan anywhere."

Meg and Kerry smiled shyly. "How do you do, Miss Mariah," they both said.

The elderly lady looked them over carefully. "You both look very nice," she said. "And now you must meet Paris."

Meg and Kerry were beside her in an instant. Both girls were much too old to play with dolls, but this doll was different. Paris was part of a mystery!

"Your doll is beautiful," Meg said. "Is she very old?"

"Indeed she is," Miss Mariah answered. "Paris is one of the first talking dolls ever made. Paris is ancient"—Mariah's blue eyes twinkled merrily— "just like me."

Laughing softly, she made room for Meg and Kerry to sit beside her on the sofa. But when she turned to Lucy, the elderly lady's smile was gone. "Sit down, Lucy," she said. "I want to tell you about Paris—and other things."

Lucy raised her eyebrows, rather surprised. She moved a low chair close to the sofa and sat down. "Yes, Miss Mariah?" she said.

For a long moment Miss Mariah remained silent, stroking Paris's soft hair.

"I know the people in town think I'm a bit odd," she said at last. "I have only myself to blame for that. But you have always been my good friend, Lucy, and I think the time has come to explain things to

27

you. I'm old now, and I'm worried, and my secret bothers me more every day."

A secret! Meg reached for Kerry's hand and squeezed it. Kerry's blue eyes were shining like stars, and her nose wiggled with curiosity.

Impatiently Mariah shook her thin shoulders and looked Lucy straight in the eye. "There's something very strange going on around here," she said firmly. "And that's why I've decided to tell you my story today. I don't know where to begin, so . . . I'll start with Paris."

Miss Mariah sat up a little straighter and moved the doll on her knee. "Paris was my mother's doll before she was mine," she began. "Mother's father, Ben Higgins, bought the doll in Paris, France. That's why he named her Paris. She was an unusual doll at that time. Her eyes open and close, and her body is made of soft kidskin. She used to say 'Mamma' when you tipped her forward, but not anymore. Paris has never spoken since that awful day."

Meg and Kerry exchanged puzzled looks, but they didn't say a word.

"I was only six years old when my parents died," Miss Mariah went on. "I came here to River House to live with my grandfather. He gave me my mother's doll to welcome me to his home, and I have had Paris ever since."

Kerry clapped her hands with delight. "That's

why you always carry Paris with you!'' she exclaimed.

Their hostess shook her head. ''No, not exactly, Kerry.'' She sighed, then went on. ''Granddaddy and I were very close. 'The Colonel' was my playmate as well as my parent—''

''The Colonel?'' Lucy broke in quickly.

Miss Mariah smiled, remembering days long past. '' 'The Colonel' was a family nickname for Ben Higgins,'' she explained. ''Granddaddy had been an army officer for a time, and he had a very military manner about him. The family and his close friends called him 'the Colonel.' Outsiders didn't know this, of course, and I'd rather you didn't mention it now.''

Lucy nodded. ''As you wish,'' she said.

''River House was a busy plantation in those days,'' Miss Mariah continued. ''Granddaddy and I rode horseback through the fields and down to the river every day to oversee the work. One day, as a surprise, he took me up to the old playroom and gave me all my mother's toys.''

Miss Mariah leaned back against the sofa cushion and closed her eyes, a shadow of a smile flickering on her lips. ''Everything in the playroom belonged to me, except Mercy and Charity,'' she said slowly. ''They were the two little wooden dolls that were kept in a glass cabinet. They weren't pretty dolls— they had been made from wooden clothespins. Their faces and hair had been painted on the knobs. Charity

29

was the serious doll. Her hair was black, and she wore a long black dress and a blue shawl. Mercy had a happy face and yellow hair. Her dress was gray and her shawl was white. These two dolls belonged to Granddaddy.''

Miss Mariah's voice trembled, and she bent her head, pretending to readjust Paris on her knee. But Meg had seen the tears in her eyes. When Miss Mariah looked up, she was calm and composed again.

"Granddaddy had given the clothespin dolls to my mother when she was small," the elderly lady told them. "But later, he decided the little dolls were much too valuable to give to me. I was not allowed to touch the clothespin dolls."

Meg leaned forward eagerly. "But why, Miss Mariah?" she asked. "What was it that made the dolls so valuable?"

Mariah Collins shook her head. "I don't know, Meg," she sighed. "I used to look at those little dolls in the glass case and wonder how two such homely dolls could be so priceless. Granddaddy always said he would explain someday, but. . . ."

A look of sadness clouded Miss Mariah's eyes, and she drew a deep breath. "Forty-two years ago today, Granddaddy turned eighty-five years old," she went on. "He was a handsome old gentleman. He was strong and healthy and still rode his horse about the plantation. He was proud of his age, and, to celebrate, he gave a party for the family and close friends.

"My cousin Florabelle brought her two small children to the party. Sonny was six; Jane was four. They were allowed to go upstairs to the old playroom."

Mariah shook her head, remembering that day. "Well," she said, "there was a quarrel—and those two children wrecked the playroom. They broke the toys, smashed the dollhouse, and pulled the arms and legs off Paris! Poor thing, she has never spoken another word. But worst of all"—the elderly lady's eyes flashed—"Granddaddy's two wooden dolls were lost."

Meg's eyes grew even darker with interest. "Then what happened?" she asked.

Miss Mariah looked distressed. "My granddaddy was outraged," she said. "He sent the guests home. And he ordered Cousin Florabelle and her children to leave the house and never return."

Miss Mariah's mouth tightened into a thin, straight line. "I have never seen or heard from Cousin Florabelle and her children from that day to this," she said.

Meg was growing excited. "Did you ever find the two wooden dolls?" she asked quickly.

Miss Mariah smiled sadly. "My grandfather did,

31

Meg,'' she answered. "All the excitement was too much for me. I became very ill, and I was in bed for weeks. The medicine my doctor gave me kept me dull and sleepy. I dozed and woke, then dozed again. All the days ran together in a jumble. I have never been able to get things clear. If I could only remember all that happened. . . .''

Frowning, Mariah rubbed her forehead, trying to find the answer. "I can remember Granddaddy's visits to my room every day,'' she said, almost speaking to herself. "I remember he told me he was busy fixing the playroom and the broken toys. And then, one day, he came in and gave Paris to me. 'There she is, Mariah,' he said. 'She can't talk now, but maybe someday she will. Keep listening.' ''

Again Mariah's smile was sad. "And then, I remember, Granddaddy laughed and told me he had found his two little dolls,'' she said. "And he said he had hidden them both away again.''

Kerry gave a gasp. Meg's heart skipped a beat.

"Where?'' Meg asked. "Where did he say he had hidden the dolls?''

The elderly lady shook her head slowly. "I can't remember, Meg,'' she sighed. "I was very sick that day. I had been given a great deal of medicine, and I was groggy.''

Miss Mariah closed her eyes, trying to find her way back to that long-ago day with her grandfather.

"I could hear Granddaddy's voice, going on and on. He must have been telling me exactly where he had put the two dolls and how to find them," she said. "But I felt so tired and sleepy . . . I kept dozing. . . ."

Miss Mariah sighed deeply. "The next thing I knew, Granddaddy was saying, 'It won't be easy, Mariah, but you'll find them. Turn the house upside down, and you'll find them.' And then he chuckled as he said, 'Mercy and Charity will be safe now. You and I are the only ones in the world who know where they are.' "

Meg touched the old lady's arm gently. "But where did your grandfather say he put them?" she asked again.

"That's all I can remember, Meg," Miss Mariah said. "I've tried and tried, all these years, but I cannot remember where Granddaddy told me he put the clothespin dolls.

"I was too ill to ask any questions that day," she went on, "and I thought there would be plenty of time to do that later."

Miss Mariah bent her head, hiding her face. "After lunch that day, Granddaddy decided to ride around the plantation. It was his first ride since the birthday party, and it was to be his last ride."

Her voice shook, and her eyes grew misty. "His horse stumbled, and he was thrown to the ground. He died instantly."

Quick tears sparkled in Meg's eyes.

Mariah raised her head. "Granddaddy's death made me very bitter," she said softly. "I blamed his death on the toys. I felt he had worked too hard fixing them, and I hated them—all except Paris. I felt she was a part of Granddaddy, and I vowed to keep her with me. But I never wanted to see the other toys again. I locked the playroom door, and I've kept it locked ever since."

Kerry was too excited to remember her manners. "Is that the locked room you go to visit every afternoon?" she asked.

The question surprised Miss Mariah, and she seemed amused. "I see there are no secrets in Williamsburg." She smiled. "Yes, Kerry, that's the room. I finally got over my foolish idea. The toys had nothing at all to do with my grandfather's death. One day I went into the old playroom. The room was neat and orderly; the toys were patched and mended, just as Granddaddy had left them. But the glass cabinet looked empty and lonely without the two wooden dolls." Miss Mariah sighed. "I have searched this house from top to bottom, over and over again, looking for those two little dolls. But—"

"You never found them," Meg said sadly.

"I never found them," Miss Mariah repeated.

Lucy took the little lady's hands in hers. "I'm sure the dolls must be here someplace," she said gently.

Miss Mariah squeezed Lucy's hands. For one quick moment, Meg thought she looked frightened. "Lucy," Mariah said, "I know you are still wondering why I have told you this story. I have a very good reason. I must go away on business next week, and I want you to take my toys to your toy show."

Leaning closer, Mariah spoke very softly. "I'm worried, Lucy," she said. "I believe someone is trying to steal my old toys."

3
THE SECRET ROOM

"But how could anyone steal your toys, Miss Mariah?" Meg asked. "Nobody knows about them."

"Except us," Kerry added.

Their hostess frowned. "That's very true," she admitted. "But, somehow, some people have found out about them. Lately several young men have come here, asking about my family and the plantation—and they all have wanted to know if I have any old toys."

"How strange," Lucy said.

Out in the hall, a clock struck the hour. Miss Mariah stood up and tucked Paris under her arm. "It's three o'clock," she said. "We'll have to hurry. I'm going to take you upstairs to see the toys. The playroom is very dark when the sunlight is gone. There are no electric lights there, you know."

Meg and Kerry looked at each other and grinned.

They were both thinking the same thing.

"Is that the reason you always go up to the locked room between two and three o'clock?" Meg asked.

Miss Mariah's blue eyes twinkled. "Exactly, Meg. It's not so mysterious, after all, is it?"

Turning, she led the way upstairs to the playroom. The door squeaked a little as Miss Mariah pushed it open and stepped inside.

Sunshine poured through the small panes of glass in the window, lighting the big attic room. Meg thought it was a lovely room. She loved the beauty of old woods and handmade things.

Standing in the doorway, she looked around the playroom. Thick wooden beams supported the ceiling. One of the walls sloped way down low to the floor. At the bottom of the sloping wall, Meg noticed a little door, almost like a trapdoor.

"Miss Mariah, what's behind that little door?" she asked.

Miss Mariah laughed softly. "That's my 'secret room,' Meg," she answered. "It's really only a crawl space that goes back under the roof to the chimney. My grandfather often hid presents in there; he called it the 'secret room.' "

Mariah's smile faded into a frown. "It was the first place I looked when I began my search for the dolls," she said. "Somehow, I was sure I would find them in the secret room, but I didn't." Miss Mariah

37

turned away from the trapdoor. "I still can't help feeling that someday the dolls may be found in the secret room. And that's why I have kept the playroom door locked all these years."

Kerry and Lucy were down on the floor looking at the toys. Meg sat down with them.

The old toys were in fine condition. A child's table was set with tiny china dishes and real linen. A floppy rag doll slept in a toy cradle. There were some books and some stuffed animals. But the dollhouse was the toy that impressed everyone most. "How beautiful!" Lucy murmured.

The toy house was painted white, with big, tall columns holding up the roof of the wide front veranda. Thick twin chimneys of tiny red bricks stood on each side of the house. Meg knew the design at once. "Miss Mariah! This is River House," she cried.

Miss Mariah nodded. "That's right," she said, pleased. "Granddaddy built this little house himself. He used the original plans of the family plantation. Every room in the dollhouse is exactly as it is in the big house."

Meg and Kerry both looked inside the dollhouse. Meg smiled when she saw the playroom on the top floor. "Even the little trapdoor is here in the playroom wall," she said, delighted. "Everything is just perfect!" She squinted her eyes and leaned back to

study the house more carefully. "Did you know that the roof is crooked?" she asked. She put out her hand to touch it.

"Don't touch it, Meg," Miss Mariah said quickly. "That's the way Granddaddy fixed it, and I want it left that way."

Lucy went to hug her old friend. "Mariah, I had no idea you had things like these tucked away," she said. "These toys are delightful! The dollhouse is the most beautiful I've ever seen. It will be the hit of the toy show. Of course I'll use your toys. And we won't say where we got them."

A tiny smile slipped across the elderly lady's face. "Thank you, Lucy," she said softly. "It will be a great comfort to know the toys are safe at the exhibition. The servants will be here at the house, of course, but I just wouldn't have felt easy about leaving the toys here." Mariah patted Lucy's hand. "Now I won't have to worry."

She looked down at the two girls on the floor. "I want to tell you something, Margaret Ashley Duncan," she said. "Your mother and Lucy were the only ones I ever allowed to hold Paris. I know I can trust you and Kerry to take good care of my toys. They aren't worth much money, but they mean a great deal to me. Will you promise to take good care of them for me?"

Both Meg and Kerry nodded their heads. "Yes, Miss Mariah," they answered in one voice.

Leaning down, Mariah Collins placed Paris in Meg's arms. "Carry her as carefully as your mother used to, Meg," she said, smiling softly.

"Oh, I will," Meg promised.

Mariah looked pleased. "Good," she said. "Be sure not to handle her roughly, Meg. Paris is very old and fragile, you know."

Then, quickly, Mariah turned and walked to the door. "Now, let's gather up these toys and get them out to the station wagon. I'm afraid it's going to rain."

With everybody helping, it took only a few minutes to get the toys out into the hall. Just as they were ready to start downstairs, the doorbell rang.

Miss Mariah looked annoyed. "I'm not expecting anyone. The housekeeper has gone downtown, and there's no one downstairs to answer the door."

"I'll get it," Meg offered.

Holding Paris, she flew down the stairs to the front door.

"Yes?" she said as she opened the door.

The young man who stood there looked startled. "Oh—er, hi," he said. "My name is Stephen Anderson. Are—are you the lady of the house?"

"Of course not, silly," Meg said, giggling.

The young man smiled nervously. "It was the long dress that fooled me," he said. "Do you always dress like that?"

"This is a costume," Meg explained. "I'm a junior hostess at the toy show next week. Paris and I will both be there."

"Paris?" Stephen's eyes widened as he noticed the doll in Meg's arms. "Is that doll called Paris?"

He stepped inside the big hall. "Look," he said excitedly, "is there a place around here called River House?"

"This is River House," Meg answered.

"No kidding!" Stephen cried. "Would you be Miss Mariah Collins?" he teased.

"No, young man." Miss Mariah spoke from the

stairs. Her voice was cold and unfriendly. "She is not Mariah Collins. I am."

Stephen's face turned red. "Oh, uh—" he stammered. "Miss Mariah—"

"Miss Collins," the elderly lady corrected him.

The young man swallowed. "Er—of course—Miss Collins," he began again. "My name is—"

Mariah closed her eyes and held her hand up for silence. "Young man, I don't care who you are or where you came from. You are here without invitation, and I must ask you to leave."

Stephen looked even more embarrassed than before and left at once.

"Who was that?" Lucy asked, coming down the last few steps.

"A rude young man, like all those other strangers that have come here, asking questions," Miss Mariah said with a tired sigh. "I'll have nothing at all to do with any of them."

She walked over to the front door and looked outside. "Hurry now, Lucy, and pack the toys. It's beginning to rain."

The toys were brought down quickly and loaded into the station wagon. The dollhouse was the last thing to be put in. It took all three of them to handle it. Very carefully Meg and Kerry helped Lucy slide the dollhouse into the back of the wagon.

Miss Mariah stood in the doorway and waved

good-bye as Lucy drove down the driveway. Meg thought the elderly little lady looked lonesome, seeing her old toys being taken away.

Lucy was delighted as she thought of the treasures behind her in the station wagon. "I can't believe it!" she said. "We have Paris and all the rest of Miss Mariah's toys."

"Not quite," Meg said. "The two wooden dolls are lost." She looked serious. "I wonder what made those wooden dolls so valuable," she said slowly. "Clothespin dolls aren't very special. But the Colonel kept his clothespin dolls in a special glass cabinet. I wonder why. . . ."

Kerry's little pixie nose wrinkled, the way it always did when she was excited. "It's real mysterious, isn't it?" she said.

Lucy burst out laughing. "Hal Ashley was right," she chuckled. "He told me you kids dig up a mystery everyplace you go."

Meg and Kerry laughed with her.

"We always solve the mystery, too," Kerry said.

Meg only smiled. She couldn't stop thinking how nice it would be if they could help Miss Mariah find the lost clothespin dolls.

Lucy slowed the station wagon and pointed ahead. "Look at that young fellow walking in the rain," she said. "He'll be soaked!"

"Why, that's Stephen Anderson, the boy who

43

came to Miss Mariah's house," Meg said, surprised. "Could we give him a ride, Lucy?" she asked.

Lucy frowned. "We don't really know much about him, Meg," she said. "I don't like to pick up a stranger on the road."

"He's not really a stranger," Meg pointed out quickly. "I wasn't very nice to him, and if we could give him a ride, it might make up for that."

"Okay," Lucy said. She pulled over to the side of the road and stopped the car. "Ask him if he wants a ride."

Meg didn't need to ask. Stephen was inside the station wagon almost the second the car stopped.

"Oh, boy, thanks," he said, settling into the backseat. "I was afraid I'd drown out there, waiting for a bus back to Williamsburg."

Meg turned around to face him. "Hi, Stephen," she said.

"Well, hello again," Stephen said, grinning. "Hope you and Paris didn't get wet."

Lucy's eyebrows shot up in surprise. "How did you know this doll is called Paris?" she asked.

Meg answered Lucy's question. "I told him," she said. "But I forgot to tell him my own name." Quickly Meg made the introductions.

Sprawled in the backseat, Stephen looked around at the toys. "You sure have a lot of old toys back here," he said.

He bent over to get a closer look. Suddenly he seemed excited. "You didn't tell me you had Miss Mariah's old dollhouse, Meg," he said. "What's the matter with the roof? It's crooked."

Nobody answered him. Meg stole a glance sideways. She could see Lucy was upset.

"Do you live here in town, Stephen?" Lucy asked. Her voice was strained.

"No, I'm just visiting," Stephen answered. We're staying downtown, at a motel. I've never been to Williamsburg before, but my fa—" He stopped short, suddenly uneasy. "I'll only be here a few days," he finished.

A few minutes later Lucy pulled up in front of her little house. Meg looked for Uncle Hal's roadster, but it wasn't parked at the curb.

"Uncle Hal's not back yet," she said.

Lucy sighed. "That means we have a problem," she said. "We'll have to use the chimney door, and I'm not sure we'll be able to handle that dollhouse."

Stephen offered at once to help. "If Meg and Kerry walk backward and hold one end, I can manage the other end," he said.

Lucy hesitated for only a minute. "Okay," she said. "I'll carry Paris."

Carefully they lifted the heavy dollhouse and carried it around to the chimney door.

"Now, be careful coming through this doorway,"

Lucy warned as she stepped inside. "The opening is very narrow, and it'll be a tight squeeze."

Meg and Kerry tightened their grips and backed through the doorway, easing the heavy dollhouse past the narrow wooden frame. Meg sighed with relief when she felt the dirt floor of the woodshed under her feet. "We're almost there," she called to Stephen. "Keep coming."

"Okay," he replied.

Just as he stepped through the doorway, a sudden gust of wind swung the door up hard against his back. Stephen felt himself falling. "Watch out!" he shouted.

"Ooooh!" Kerry squealed, feeling the dollhouse slip.

"Hold it, Kerry! Hold it!" Meg cried.

Frantically the girls tried to balance their burden, but the heavy dollhouse slid out of their hands and crashed to the floor.

The chimney door blew closed with a loud bang, and suddenly the old woodshed was pitch-black.

4

WHERE'S PARIS?

"Don't move, anybody!" Lucy's voice sounded hollow in the dark woodshed. "I'll open the door."

A moment later, pale light streamed in from the open living room door. It barely reached the middle of the old shed, but they all saw the dollhouse.

"Oh, thank goodness!" Meg breathed a sigh of relief. "It landed right side up," she said.

"Bring it into the living room," Lucy said. "The shed is too dark to see it very well."

Nothing appeared to be wrong with the little house. Although Meg and Kerry hadn't been strong enough to stop the house from falling, they had broken much of the force of the fall. Some of the tiny furniture had bounced around, but nothing was broken.

Stephen was embarrassed. "I'm awfully sorry," he said. "It was my fault. The door hit me, and, as usual, I tripped over my big feet.'' He grinned self-consciously and looked down at his brown loafers. ''I have awfully big feet,'' he sighed.

''It wasn't your fault at all,'' Lucy said kindly. ''Blame it on the wind.''

Meg was very quiet as she walked around the dollhouse, looking at it from all angles. Her artist's eye had seen something the others hadn't noticed. ''I think the fall improved the dollhouse,'' she said finally. ''The roof is straight now.''

Lucy seemed surprised. ''Are you sure?'' she asked. ''Why, Miss Mariah said that roof had been crooked for years and years.''

''I wonder what happened,'' Kerry said.

Meg grinned. ''I think I know,'' she said. She ran her fingers along the edge of the roof, feeling for something. ''Lots of dollhouses are made so the roof lifts off. Then the children can reach inside and play with the furniture.''

Lucy shook her head. ''No, Meg,'' she said. ''The windows and doors of this little house open, but the roof stays in place. Old-fashioned children were content just to look at things. I'm sure Ben Higgins didn't make this roof removable.''

Stephen was leaning against the mantel, viewing the dollhouse from a distance. ''That roof is as straight as an arrow now,'' he said. ''Something must have been pushing it crooked. Then, when we

48

dropped the house, the roof flew up and then settled back down in place again, just like that.''

He grinned, rather pleased with himself. ''Now I have to get back to my motel. It's almost five o'clock.''

''Good heavens,'' Lucy said. ''I'd better start dinner. We have to go to Brush-Everard House tonight, and we'll never make it if I don't hurry.''

She smiled at Stephen. ''Thanks for helping,'' she said. ''Meg and Kerry will show you out.''

As soon as Stephen left, the girls changed into working clothes. Dressed in blue jeans and sneakers, they ran out to the car to bring in the rest of Miss Mariah's toys. It had stopped raining, but the trees showered them with ice-cold raindrops, and they had to jump over mud puddles.

''I wonder why Uncle Hal isn't here yet,'' Meg said as she stepped carefully around a small puddle. ''He should be back by now.''

Kerry brushed a raindrop from her hair. ''Don't worry about him,'' she said. ''He'll be here soon.''

Meg hoped so. She had so much to tell him! But when Lucy called the girls to dinner, Uncle Hal still hadn't returned.

Meg was worried as she and Kerry dressed to go uptown. It wasn't like Uncle Hal to be so late. She couldn't stop wondering what was keeping him.

Kerry could see that Meg was upset. ''Maybe he

had a flat tire or something like that," she guessed.

"Mmm, maybe," Meg sighed. "I'll just leave a note in his room, saying we're going uptown. He'll find us."

Kerry pulled on her white sweater. "Okay," she said. "Want me to take Paris?"

Meg glanced at Paris. The doll was sitting in a little rocking chair, looking like a tiny old-fashioned child.

"No, just leave her there," Meg answered, beginning to scribble her note. "I'll bring her along with me in a minute."

Meg wrote the short note quickly on a page from her sketching pad. Then she hurried into her uncle's room. She pushed the note under the mirror frame, beside the newspaper clipping she had left there that afternoon. The man in the picture seemed to be watching her, and Meg giggled nervously. "Good night, whoever you are," she said.

She tucked her sketching pad and pencil into her pocket. Taking Paris, Meg ran downstairs to join Kerry and Lucy.

The wide Duke of Gloucester Street was still shiny from the rain. Lights glowed in the windows of the old houses, making shimmering patches of gold on the red brick sidewalks. Behind the picket fences, Meg could see quaint gardens of spring flowers.

Lucy pointed out the old buildings as they walked

along the street. When they came to the Raleigh Tavern, Meg stopped to look at the big white house with the neat black shutters. It didn't look much like a hotel, but Meg knew the old tavern had once been the best hotel in town. She could picture George Washington tying his horse to the hitching post; she could see Thomas Jefferson hurrying up to the front door on his way to a meeting; she could even hear Patrick Henry's golden voice ringing out in protest.

"This is a beautiful old house," Meg said as she took her sketching pad out of her pocket. "Could we stop here for a little while? I'd like to make a sketch of the tavern for Daddy."

Lucy agreed. "That will please your father, Meg," she said. "I'll hold Paris for you."

As Meg started to hand the doll to Lucy, she remembered something. "Kerry and I promised Miss Mariah we would take care of her toys," she said thoughtfully, "so perhaps Kerry should hold Paris." She handed the doll to Kerry.

Meg wasted no time beginning her sketch. Her pencil zigzagged over the paper with quick, clever strokes. Lucy watched closely.

"Kerry, run into the Raleigh Tavern Bakery and get us some ginger cookies," Lucy said quietly. "I'll stay here with Meg."

"Sure," Kerry said, taking the money that Lucy handed her.

52

There were no other customers in the bakery. Kerry stood close to the long counter and watched the bakers sliding big trays of bread dough into the red brick ovens.

One tall baker slid a tray of hot bread onto the counter top. He didn't see Kerry standing there. The hot tray touched her fingers.

Kerry jumped. "Ouch!" she cried, grabbing her burnt fingers with her other hand. Paris toppled over on the counter.

Obviously upset by the mishap, the baker said, "Oh, I'm so sorry! Come back here and let me fix that burn."

Kerry hesitated. She didn't know what to do with Paris. "I guess she'll be all right here on the counter for a minute," she said. She followed the baker around behind the big ovens.

While the baker fixed her burn, a large group of people came into the shop. They all bought ginger cookies, which seemed to be a specialty of the shop. Kerry was sure there wouldn't be one ginger cookie left for her.

"Do you have any more ginger cookies?" she asked as soon as the crowd had gone.

The tall baker smiled. "We always have ginger cookies, young lady," he said. "You can have as many as you can carry."

Kerry giggled. "I can't carry many this time,"

53

she laughed. "I'm wounded, and I have to carry Paris, and—" All of a sudden she stopped talking, and her eyes widened. "Paris!" she cried, looking along the counter and on the floor. "Oh, golly, where is she?"

"Hey there," another baker called. "Are you looking for that old doll that was on the counter?"

Kerry nodded excitedly. "Yes, I am," she said. "Where is she?"

"Some young fella picked her up and went out," the baker told her. "I thought the little doll belonged to him, so I didn't say anything."

Kerry sighed with relief. "That must have been Mr. Ashley. He'll be outside with my friends."

Taking the bag of ginger cookies, Kerry left the old bakery.

Meg and Lucy were standing in front of the tavern, where Kerry had left them. Meg's head was still bent low over her drawing.

"Here I am," Kerry called. "Where's Mr. Ashley?"

Meg went on sketching. "Uncle Hal?" she asked, surprised. "He's not here."

Kerry's pixie face crumpled. "But—but didn't he come out here with Paris?" she asked shakily.

Meg looked up at once. "Kerry!" she said, noticing Kerry's empty arms. "Where's Paris?"

Lucy turned pale. Very gently she put her arms around Kerry and said, "Tell us what happened."

5
FOOTSTEPS ON THE STAIRS

". . . and so," Kerry finished her story in a rush, "I thought Mr. Ashley would be out here, waiting for me."

Meg was very serious. "Kerry," she said, "I'm afraid someone has stolen Miss Mariah's old doll!"

Lucy forced a smile, but her voice also was serious. "Now, let's try not to get excited," she said. "Someone probably picked up Paris by mistake. I'm sure whoever took her will bring her right back here to the bakery when he realizes what has happened."

Lucy turned quickly and walked away so that Meg and Kerry wouldn't see the worried look on her face. "I'll leave my phone number at the bakery," she called back over her shoulder. "I'll tell them we'll be at Brush-Everard House for a while, too."

Miserable and unhappy, Kerry watched Lucy go into the bakeshop. "This is all my fault," she sniffled.

Meg's eyes were troubled. *Why would anyone steal Paris?* she asked herself silently. She was just an old doll, too fragile to play with—and not worth a lot of money.

Meg squared her chin and put a comforting arm around Kerry. Somehow they *had* to find Paris.

It was getting dark when they finally reached Brush-Everard House. Small and cozy and painted the color of mustard, the house stood at the far end of Palace Green, next to the stately Governor's Palace.

Lucy stopped at the side gate. "We have to use the back door," she said. "Visiting hours are over, and the house is closed to the public for the day. I want you kids to see the Child's Room and the toys. Then we'll rehearse your parts for the toy show."

Opening the gate, Lucy led the way down the side path and around to the back door. A wave of cool air hit their faces when the door was opened. They all stepped inside.

A narrow, steep flight of worn wooden stairs, leading up to the Child's Room, stretched before them. The stairs were closed in by two solid walls. It was so dark that Meg could barely see where she was going. She was glad when she stepped out into the Child's Room.

The room was quite tiny. It was almost like an alcove at one end of the big northeast bedroom. The sloping walls were painted white. A window looked out on a garden, and another doorway led into the big bedroom. The wooden floor was bare, and the furniture was simple: a single bed, a baby's cradle, and one wooden chair.

Lucy opened the wooden blind at the window, letting in the soft glow of twilight. "That back stairway is kept closed to all visitors," she said, "but it's the quickest way to get to this room. The Child's Room is so small that no one is allowed to enter it. That's the reason we keep the rope across the doorway. The visitors stand in the big bedroom and look in here through that door."

Meg looked about the room. "Oh, I see," she said. "The Child's Room is almost like a stage—and the audience stands out there, in the next room."

"Exactly," Lucy said, nodding. "Now, let's look at the toys."

Over in a corner, there were two boxes filled with old toys for the show. Meg and Kerry sat on the floor and began to unpack them.

One box held tiny wooden carts, brightly painted wooden soldiers, and several hand-carved wooden trains. There was even a wooden jigsaw puzzle.

Meg reached into the second box and lifted out a hand puppet. "Look at this, Kerry," she cried. "It's

57

Punch!'' The next second she pulled out the Judy puppet.

Kerry studied the intricately carved wooden puppets, then dipped her hand into the box and pulled out a gaily costumed marionette. It was worked by countless thread-slender strings.

"Wow!" Kerry said. "How did anyone ever keep all the strings straight?"

Lucy laughed. "That marionette belonged to a professional performer," she said. "He went around to all the theaters giving shows. Punch and Judy were brought here from England. Puppet shows have a long history, you know. They're so old that nobody really knows when they started. They used to be very popular. Some of our greatest writers and composers wrote shows for puppets."

Kerry removed a group of small dolls from the box. They were all exactly the same size, but each doll was dressed in a different style.

"That's a set of fashion dolls, Kerry," Lucy pointed out. "People traveling in Europe used to bring those little dolls back to the Colonies to show the ladies the newest fashions."

Kerry grinned when she heard that. "I bet they were popular," she said.

Meg held up a floppy old rag doll. "Look at this one," she said.

The doll's arms and legs were yellow with age,

58

and her dress was worn. But her yarn hair was still as red as a tomato, and her faded smile was as wide and happy as it was the day she was born.

"That's Jelly Bean," Lucy said. "She was made by five sisters, and they gave her a red jelly bean for her heart. According to one story, her dress was made from a piece of an English queen's dress."

Meg gave the doll a little shake. Jelly Bean flopped loosely, this way and that. "She's nice and soft," Meg said.

"That's probably why the little girls loved her so," Lucy said. "All dolls used to be wooden, and little girls couldn't cuddle them. Soft dolls didn't appear until the French started to make dolls. They gave their dolls soft kid bodies. The French were also the first ones to make dolls that opened and closed their eyes and dolls that talked."

Meg looked thoughtful. "Just like Paris," she said slowly.

Kerry caught her breath. "Maybe Paris is more valuable than Miss Mariah realizes!" Kerry exclaimed. "Maybe that's why somebody stole her!"

Suddenly the happy feeling was gone from the room. Lucy's frown was deep and very worried as she put her arms around the girls.

"I hate to say this, kids," she said slowly, "but I'm beginning to think that maybe someone did steal Paris. Maybe it would be best to report it to the police when we leave here. We can rehearse your parts tomorrow.''

''Shhh!'' Meg held her finger to her lips. ''Someone is on the back stairs,'' she whispered.

Kerry looked frightened. She moved up close to Meg. Standing there, in the dimly lighted room, they strained their ears, listening. They could hear someone creeping up the old dark stairway.

Step by step, the sound grew louder. Then it stopped. Meg could tell that the ''someone'' was standing at the top of the stairs.

''Who is it?'' Meg shaped the words silently with her lips.

''Shhh,'' Lucy whispered. ''They're going downstairs now.''

The footsteps, still soft but more rapid now, grew fainter, and the next minute they all heard the back door being closed, very quietly. The ''someone'' was gone.

Lucy rushed over to the window. Meg and Kerry raced to the door and looked out on the dark stairway.

There, propped up against the doorframe, was Paris!

''Lucy! Look!'' Meg picked up the doll and ran back into the room.

Amazed, Lucy took the old doll from Meg's arms. ''Is she broken or anything?'' she asked.

All three of them bent to examine Miss Mariah's old doll. Paris's arms and legs still moved, and her clothes weren't torn. Nothing seemed to be broken.

Lucy smiled with relief. "Thank goodness Paris is safe!" she said. "Whoever picked her up must have returned her to the bakery. One of the bakers probably brought her over here. They knew we were coming here. At any rate, we've had enough excitement for one evening," she said. "We're going home."

Outside, the street was dark and quiet and full of deep shadows. The dirt sidewalk was slippery. Meg and Kerry didn't talk much, and they stayed close to Lucy.

As soon as they turned down Lucy's street, Meg looked for Uncle Hal's car, but there was no black roadster parked at the curb. *That's funny,* she thought. *Uncle Hal's never late. Something must have happened.*

Lucy gave them milk and cookies out in the kitchen. Then it was time to go to bed. Lucy hugged them fondly. "Sleep tight," she said.

Kerry went right to her room. Meg decided to go to Uncle Hal's bedroom to turn down the covers.

As she put Paris down on the dresser, she looked for the note she had left in the mirror frame. The note was gone! And the man in the newspaper clipping no longer stared out at her.

Slightly bewildered, Meg turned down the covers

and went off to her own room. There she found a note pinned to her pillow.

> Maggie-me-love,
> Got your note. Sorry to have missed you. Something important has come up, and I can't say when I'll be back. Expect me when you see me. I'll explain later. You and Kerry have fun—and be careful, Maggie.
>
>   Uncle Hal

Meg was smiling as she climbed into bed.

6
THE TOY SHOW

Long before Kerry was awake the next morning, Meg slipped out of bed. She was used to being alone, and she liked to have "thinking time" in the quiet of early morning. Meg had a lot of things to think about today.

Paris sat in the doll rocker beside the bed, where Meg had left her. The little doll looked very prim and sedate. Meg tiptoed across the room to get her sketching pad. Then she picked up the little doll and examined it. Paris's china head wobbled slightly, and Meg frowned when she felt the thick seam down the doll's back.

Very slowly Meg bent Paris forward, hoping she might hear a faint "Mamma." But there wasn't the slightest sound.

"The Colonel didn't do a very good job putting you back together," Meg said as she set the doll back in her rocking chair. Seconds later, Meg's pencil was moving rapidly over her paper.

"Paris," she asked softly as she worked, "what really happened to you last night? Did someone steal you? Who took you from the bakeshop? And who brought you back and left you sitting out on the stairs?"

Paris's round blue eyes stared straight ahead, telling her nothing. Meg went on sketching. Line by line, the little rocking chair and the old-fashioned doll appeared on her paper.

"Come on, sleepyhead," Meg cried, sweeping the covers off Kerry. "Time to get up."

Meg and Kerry were busy all day. With Lucy's help, they wrote out their speeches to introduce the toys at the toy show. It was decided that Kerry would show the wooden toys and Miss Mariah's plantation dollhouse. Meg would show the other dolls and the puppets, along with Paris.

"People are going to love Jelly Bean," Meg chuckled as she wrote down the story of the rag doll's candy heart.

Kerry was very serious. "I think I'll tell how a plantation was run in Colonial days," she said. "Plantations were almost like small towns. The people grew or made everything they needed."

After the speeches were written, they rehearsed

them aloud with Lucy. Meg had little trouble. She had appeared in dance recitals and was used to having an audience.

But Kerry was nervous. "It's much harder than riding a horse," she said.

Lucy laughed. "Relax, Kerry," she said. "Remember, the audience is there to listen to you, not to frighten you. And don't try to memorize your talk word for word. Know what you want to say, and then go ahead and say it. Talk to your audience as if you were talking to a friend."

Kerry blinked and took a deep breath. "Okay," she said. "I'll try again."

It wasn't long before she was giving her talks as easily as Meg.

After dinner, workmen came to get Miss Mariah's toys. Lucy went over to Brush-Everard House to set up the show. Sunday night they took a Candlelight Tour of the craft shops. When Lucy suggested an early bedtime, Meg and Kerry were more than willing to agree.

It was quite early when Lucy drove them around to Brush-Everard House on Monday morning. Meg carried Paris. Kerry carried their lunch. They had decided to take sandwiches instead of walking home to eat.

Lucy looked at the clock on the dashboard. "It's

only eight-thirty," she said. "You're early."

Meg was very businesslike. "We wanted to be early," she said. "We're going to go over our speeches again, before the visitors arrive."

Lucy started the motor. "Well, I won't keep you, then. Good luck, kids. See you tonight."

Meg and Kerry were racing down the side path before Lucy had turned her car around. Unlocking the back door, Kerry ran up the steep stairway two steps at a time.

Meg stopped to gather up her long skirt so she wouldn't trip over it. Sunlight poured in the back door. As Meg stepped on the first stair, she saw the footprints. They were big, muddy footprints, dried and yellow. There were two sets of them. One set went up the left side; the other went down the right.

Meg flew up the stairs to the Child's Room. "Kerry, come out here," she cried. "I want to show you something."

Kerry was puzzled when she saw the mud. "Muddy footprints," she said, frowning. "Where did the mud come from, Meg? There's no mud outside today."

Meg's dark eyes grew round. "But there was lots of mud last Saturday night," she said. "And somebody was out here on these stairs. Remember?"

"Oooh!" Kerry's pixie nose began to wrinkle. "You mean the one who brought Paris back last Saturday night left these footprints?" she asked.

Meg thought for a minute. "I don't know for sure," she said. Following the prints, Meg walked slowly down the stairs, studying each muddy spot. "We know Lucy used the front stairway yesterday, so she didn't do this. Besides, you can tell it was a man, from the size of the footprints," she went on. "Whoever he was, he had awfully big feet."

The words made both girls think of something.

"Stephen!" they said, looking at each other.

"I wonder—" Meg began. The sound of a bell stopped her. "There's the signal," she said. "The visitors are here. The toy show is open!"

The day began in a rush. Meg and Kerry were kept busy showing the old toys. They were both a little nervous at first, but it wasn't very long before Meg was enjoying herself.

Kerry, though, couldn't seem to relax, no matter how hard she tried. She looked uneasy as she waited for Meg to finish her talk about Paris.

Meg had just finished saying that Paris had had an accident and couldn't speak anymore, when Kerry saw a lady put up her hand. "Miss," the lady called, "what did the doll say before her accident?"

Kerry popped Punch over her fingers and held the hook-nosed puppet up in the air. "Mamma," she squeaked.

Everybody in the room roared with laughter.

That was the end of Kerry's stage fright. She began to have fun. She talked and laughed and answered questions like a professional.

Meg was happy about that. Several times, while Kerry chattered on and on, Meg had time to do a little sketching. She stood in the far corner of the Child's Room, making quick line drawings on her small sketching pad. She had time to do only a few quick impressions. She planned to finish them later, back at Lucy's.

Even though they enjoyed it, both girls were glad when their first working day was over. They were putting the toys back in place when Stephen arrived.

"Hi," he said. He stepped over the velvet rope at the doorway and walked into the Child's Room.

For a minute Meg and Kerry were flustered.

Shall I ask him about Paris? Meg wondered. *Should we say anything about the footprints?*

"I liked your show," Stephen broke in on her thoughts. "It's really great. I came back to get a closer look at the dollhouse." He patted Paris's head lightly as he passed. "Good to see Paris got back in time for her opening performance," he chuckled. Kneeling, Stephen looked closely at Miss Mariah's old dollhouse. "The roof is still straight," he said, almost to himself. "Now let's see what I can find inside the locked room on the top floor."

Meg started with surprise. "How do you know—" she began.

Behind Stephen's back, Kerry was waving her arms, trying to get Meg's attention. Meg walked over to her.

"Look!" Kerry whispered. She pointed to Stephen's shoes. Thick yellow mud was caked under the heels of Stephen's brown loafers!

Meg could only stare at the muddy shoes. There was no doubt about it. Stephen had taken Paris and then brought her back again!

7

MR. ADAM

Meg pushed her dinner plate away and leaned forward. "And, Lucy," she said, "there was mud all over Stephen Anderson's shoes. It was yellow, just like the muddy footprints on the back stairs."

Kerry bounced with excitement. "We think Stephen stole Paris, then brought her back again," she said.

Lucy frowned as she took a slow sip of her coffee. "It certainly does look that way," she said. "But we can't call a man guilty just because he has mud on his shoes."

"I know that." Meg looked thoughtful. "But there is something strange about Stephen. He seems to know so much about Miss Mariah."

"He even knew about the locked room on the top floor!" Kerry exclaimed.

"That's an old Williamsburg story, Kerry," Lucy said. "Everyone in town knows it."

"But Stephen doesn't live in Williamsburg," Meg pointed out quickly. "He's only visiting here for a few days."

Lucy looked worried as she nodded. "The best thing to do is to stay away from Stephen," she said. "Don't answer any of his questions. And don't let him get near Miss Mariah's toys."

She moved her chair back from the table and stood up. "I have to hurry and dress," she said, glancing at her watch. "I'm a hostess at the Candlelight Concert tonight. Would you like to come with me?"

"Not me," Kerry groaned. "I'm too tired."

Meg refused the invitation more graciously. "I think we'll just stay home and watch TV," she said.

For a moment Lucy seemed undecided. "I hate to leave you girls here alone," she said.

Meg giggled. "You sound like Mrs. Wilson," she said. "Don't worry. Kerry and I will be all right. You go get dressed. We'll do the dishes."

Meg and Kerry were in the living room, watching TV, when Lucy rushed downstairs. She was wearing a Colonial gown, and her dark hair was caught back from her face with a black velvet bow.

"You look beautiful, Lucy," Meg sighed.

Lucy bent her head graciously, accepting the compliment. Her long, full skirt swished around her ankles as she hurried across the room.

"I'm going out through the woodshed," she said. "I'm so late! If I take the shortcut through the back-yard gardens and run all the way, I'll get to the Governor's Palace before the concert begins."

"Be careful in that woodshed," Meg said.

Lucy stepped through the door. "I will," she said. "Night, kids."

A few seconds later Meg and Kerry heard a strange noise, as if a stone had hit the house. Immediately after that, they heard Lucy cry out, "Oh, no!"

Meg ran across the room and pulled open the woodshed door. Kerry was right behind her. In the dim light, they saw Lucy limping across the dark shed.

"What happened?" Meg asked anxiously.

Lucy held out her hand as she stepped back into the living room. She was carrying one of her shoes, and the heel was broken. "I don't really know what happened," she said in an annoyed voice. "I tripped—"

"Maybe you stepped on a piece of wood," Kerry guessed quickly.

Lucy smiled. "There hasn't been any wood in that shed for a long time, Kerry," she said.

Meg spoke up. "But we did hear a funny noise," she said.

Lucy began to laugh. "Old houses creak and groan all the time, Meg," she said. "You'll hear a lot of strange noises in this old house." She pulled up her long skirt and started upstairs. "I probably stepped on my dress," she sighed. "I'll go change my shoes."

She was back down and on her way again in a few minutes.

After Lucy left, Kerry settled down to watch TV. Meg decided to work on the sketches she had begun earlier that day.

The steady drone from the TV seemed far away as she worked. There were sketches of the old toys, interesting faces in the crowds of visitors, and a view of a very serious Kerry showing the plantation dollhouse. Time passed quickly, and when Meg looked up, she found that Kerry had gone upstairs to bed. Suddenly Meg was sleepy, too.

Putting her drawing things away, she turned off the TV. Just as she reached for Paris, the telephone rang.

"Hello," Meg said softly into the phone.

"Hi. This is Stephen Anderson," the voice at the other end of the line said. "Is this Meg or Kerry?"

"Meg," she answered coolly. "What do you want?"

There was no answer for a moment. Meg could hear Stephen talking to someone. When he spoke again, Stephen sounded excited. "Look, Meg," he said, "there's someone here with me who wants to see you and Kerry. There's something very important that you should know. It's kind of late, but will it be okay if we come over?"

Meg tightened her grip on Paris. "I'm sorry," she said, "but Kerry's asleep, and I'm just going to bed. Good night." She dropped the receiver back on the cradle.

Quickly Meg dimmed the lights and hurried upstairs. Two minutes later she was in bed. Her sleepy feeling was momentarily gone. The phone call bothered her, and her suspicions of Stephen grew by leaps and bounds.

Who was with Stephen tonight? Why did they want to see Kerry and me? What were they going to tell us? And who is Stephen Anderson, anyhow?

Restless, Meg turned over on her stomach and punched her pillow into a ball. "I'll tell Kerry about it in the morning," she sighed.

Suddenly, too tired to think anymore, Meg was asleep.

Meg didn't have time to tell about Stephen's phone call in the morning. Lucy overslept, and everybody was late getting up. It was a mad scramble getting ready for work.

Lucy was first to leave. Minutes later, Meg and Kerry dashed out the door and hurried down the street. They were halfway to Brush-Everard House when Meg told Kerry the news.

Kerry caught her breath. "Stephen said he knows something important?" she asked. "What do you suppose it is?"

"I don't know," she said slowly. Then she frowned. "But there was somebody there with him. I could hear them talking together. If Stephen comes in today, don't let him get near the toys."

"I won't even speak to him," Kerry said.

Turning the corner, they hurried up Palace Green, and a few minutes later, they were racing up the back stairway at Brush-Everard House. As soon as they stepped into the Child's Room, they knew someone had been there.

Some of the toys had been moved out of place. The doll's cradle was tipped over, and Jelly Bean lay on the floor, smiling up at the ceiling. Miss Mariah's dollhouse had been pulled back into the far corner of the room.

Almost afraid to look, Meg knelt beside the dollhouse. She looked at each room through the small windows. Nothing seemed to be damaged, and Meg sighed with relief.

"I guess everything is all right," she said.

Kerry knelt down to look for herself. "Maybe the janitor moved the house over here when he was sweeping," she guessed.

Meg settled Paris in her little chair. "No, Kerry," she said. "Someone came here to look at these old toys—especially the dollhouse. Whoever it was didn't have time to examine it. He must have heard us coming up the back stairs."

"Stephen!" Kerry said. "I bet—"

"Shhh," Meg warned. "Here come the visitors. Keep your eyes open for Stephen."

The crowds at the toy show were smaller today. Kerry took more time to talk and answer questions. It gave Meg a good chance to walk through the big bedroom, giving the small children a closer look at Paris. At intervals, she even had time to do some sketching.

She drew a profile of a little child and smiling face of a spry old lady. She tried a fuller sketch of a young man with a drooping moustache, reading a magazine. It was fun finding interesting faces in the crowd.

At twelve o'clock the toy show closed for lunch. It was a nice warm day, and Kerry and Meg had decided to take their sandwiches over to the Palace Gardens behind the Governor's Palace.

While Kerry got the lunch box, Meg looked over the pages of her sketch pad. When she came to the drawing of the young man with the bushy moustache, she stopped. "Kerry, did you notice this man?" she asked. "I don't know why he came to the show. I think he had his nose in his magazine all the time he was here.''

Kerry glanced at the sketch. ''Oh, sure, I saw him,'' she said. ''He came in a couple of times, I think.'' She took a closer look at the drawing and smiled. ''That's a good picture, Meg,'' she said. ''It looks exactly like him.''

Meg studied the sketch carefully. It showed a well-dressed young man leaning against the doorframe. His dark hair was rather long. A full, bushy moustache drooped over the corners of his mouth. His eyes were hidden as he read the magazine he held in his hand.

''I wonder who he is,'' Meg said to herself.

''I believe that's my picture,'' a deep voice said in a clipped British accent, ''and my name is Adam —my last name, that is.''

Turning around, Meg found herself looking at the real-life subject of her sketch. He bowed slightly and smiled. Meg noticed that the smile didn't quite reach his eyes, and, for a moment, she had a funny feeling that she had seen this man someplace before.

''I found your toy show most interesting,'' Mr. Adam was saying, ''and your talks were charming.''

Kerry grinned proudly. ''Thank you,'' she said.

''I'm glad you enjoyed it,'' Meg said politely.

Very carefully Mr. Adam rolled up his magazine and put it into his coat pocket. ''These toys are very

old, aren't they?" he said. "I can't help wondering —do all these toys belong to the same person here in town?"

"Oh, no," Kerry answered quickly. "The toys were lent to us by a lot of different families."

"I see." Mr. Adam nodded, then moved closer to the open doorway. "I wonder if I might be allowed to step inside for a closer look," he said.

Meg stepped into the doorway. "I'm sorry. Visitors aren't allowed to enter the Child's Room."

The man smiled. "Of course. I understand perfectly," he said. "Too bad. Old toys are a hobby of mine. I have a sizable collection and know quite a bit about them.

"Take that doll in your arms," he said, looking at Paris. "Beautiful little doll—a fine example of the first talking dolls, even though you tell us she doesn't speak anymore."

Mr. Adam reached over and patted Paris on her back. Then he frowned. "I say, the doll is quite lumpy, isn't she?" he said, feeling the thick back seam. "Whoever repaired this doll after her accident didn't know much about such things. A pity. The sewing is very loose and poorly done."

"That was—" Kerry began, then stopped as Meg shook her head, warning her not to say anything.

Mr. Adam turned his attention to the dollhouse. "I would say, as a guess, that this dollhouse is a copy of one of the old plantation houses around here,'' he said with a smile.

"Yes, it is,'' Kerry said, surprised. "The dollhouse is exactly like a big plantation house out on the old river road.''

Mr. Adam looked pleased. "I'm sure I've seen the very house you mean,'' he said. "As a matter of fact, I stopped in there one day to ask about old toys. I've had a bit of luck finding some delightful old things that way.

"Unfortunately, the lady of the house wasn't home,'' he went on. "The old housekeeper told me she believed some old toys had been taken off to the toy show, and—'' he chuckled—"and she didn't approve of that at all. She seemed to think they belonged back in the big house, in some room upstairs.''

Still chuckling, Mr. Adam looked at the dollhouse again. "I rather thought this toy house came from there,'' he said.

Turning his head, the man smiled at Meg. "Does the little doll come from there also?'' he asked.

Meg didn't return his smile. "Except for our talks, we're not allowed to give out any information about the toys,'' she told him. Meg hesitated. She hated to seem rude, but it was getting late. "And this is our lunch hour, Mr. Adam,'' she said. "We really have to leave now.''

The man glanced at his gold wristwatch. "I had no idea it was so late," he said. "I beg your pardon, young ladies."

Kerry spoke up quickly. "Nobody will be here while we have our lunch," she said, "but we'll be back again at one o'clock if you want to come back."

Mr. Adam smiled and bowed his head. "Thank you," he said. "I did enjoy our little talk." Still smiling, he left the room.

Kerry grabbed up the lunch box. Meg tucked Paris under her arm. "Come on," Kerry giggled. "Let's get over to the Palace Gardens before he comes back and starts asking more questions."

8

THE CLUE IN THE DOLLHOUSE

High on a hill overlooking the Palace Gardens, nibbling a sandwich, Meg sat looking down at the clipped green hedges and tall trees. The big garden was very quiet. Most visitors were at lunch, and the garden paths were almost empty—but not for Meg.

When she looked at the wide bowling green, she pictured a smiling English governor and his guests rolling their bowling balls. And the high holly maze was filled with laughing Colonial children, hopelessly lost on the twisting paths of the maze. Lost in her thoughts, Meg hardly heard Kerry's chattering.

". . . and he was really very smart," Kerry was saying as she unwrapped another sandwich.

"Who?" Meg asked, returning to the present.

"Mr. Adam," Kerry said, a bit annoyed. "He knew a lot about old toys."

Meg just smiled. "I'm not so sure he did," she

83

said. "He knew Paris was an old talking doll, but everybody who comes to the show knows that. And Mr. Adam might only have guessed that the dollhouse is a copy of a real plantation house."

Kerry took a slow bite of her sandwich while she thought about this. "Ye-es, you could be right, Meg," she said. "Come to think of it, he didn't mention any of the other toys, did he?"

Meg put her empty sandwich wrapper into the lunch box. "Look, some people are just entering the gardens," she said. "Let's watch. Maybe someone will get lost in the maze."

For the rest of their lunch hour, Meg and Kerry watched the visitors below in the gardens. Some of them wandered into the maze and quickly became lost. It was fun seeing them find their way out again. The girls didn't leave the gardens until the last minute. It was close to one o'clock when they went up the back stairway of Brush-Everard House. Kerry was the first one into the Child's Room.

"Oh, no!" she cried. "Meg! Hurry!"

Meg was right behind her. "Oh!" she gasped, looking around the room. "What happened, Kerry? Who did this?"

Miss Mariah's old dollhouse had been moved to the middle of the room. The toy furniture was spread all over the floor. The grand piano, the tiny chairs, the rose-colored sofa, the canopied beds—everything was scattered helter-skelter.

The next minute Meg and Kerry were on their knees, examining the dollhouse. Every room was empty. All the little curtains were crooked. The tiny rugs were rumpled and out of place.

Meg was too upset to speak. Her eyes stung with angry tears. Reaching inside the dollhouse, she began to put things back in place. As she moved one of the tiny rugs, something flashed and sparkled.

"What's that?" Kerry asked quickly.

Meg carefully removed the small bright object from the dollhouse. There, on her open palm, lay a man's golden cuff link. Both girls saw the engraved English initial at the same moment.

"*S,*" Kerry breathed, her eyes growing round with excitement.

"*S*—for Stephen," Meg said.

Silently Meg traced her finger over the old English *S,* trying to think. Why was Stephen searching the old dollhouse? What did he know about Miss Mariah's old toys? What was he looking for?

Kerry began to put the furniture back in the little house. Sparks flashed angrily in her blue eyes.

"The minute we get home tonight, we'll tell Lucy about this," she said. "Lucy will know how to take care of Stephen Anderson."

"No, Kerry," Meg said, shaking her head, "we can't tell Lucy. There's something very mysterious going on here. And if we tell Lucy, she might decide we're not safe here at the toy show." Meg's dark eyes shone with determination. "Stephen is after Miss Mariah's old toys—and you and I have to protect them. We promised Miss Mariah we'd take care of her toys."

"You're right," Kerry agreed. She pushed the dollhouse back in place. "Here come the visitors," she whispered. "Watch for Stephen."

There was no sign of Stephen. He didn't come to the show the next morning, either. Meg and Kerry watched each group of visitors, but Stephen never arrived.

While they ate lunch on the hill, Meg and Kerry talked about Stephen. "I was sure he'd be back today," Kerry said. "He's so fond of looking at Miss Mariah's dollhouse."

Meg looked serious, and her eyes were troubled. "I've been doing a lot of thinking about Stephen," she said. "He really must know something, Kerry. But what is it? And how does he know about River House and Paris? How come he knows Miss Mariah? She didn't know him. Who *is* Stephen Anderson? And why does he want Miss Mariah's old toys? I can't figure it out," she sighed, "but there *must* be an answer."

Before Kerry could say anything, a sudden movement down in the garden made both girls look toward the maze. Kerry was just in time to see somebody walk behind a tall hedge. "Meg!" she cried. "That was Stephen! He's down there in the maze."

Quickly Meg and Kerry walked over to the edge of the top step and looked down inside the high holly hedges. "Come out of there, Stephen," Kerry shouted. "We know you're in there."

The bushes waved and moved gently. Stephen stepped out onto the path. He looked embarrassed. "Hi, Meg—hi, Kerry," he said. He grinned sheepishly. "I think I'm lost."

Meg looked down at him with unfriendly eyes. "I don't know what you're after, Stephen Anderson," she said, "but you'd better stop annoying us. And stay away from our toy show!"

Kerry's face was growing redder and redder. "It's a good thing you didn't break any of that dollhouse furniture!" she cried.

Stephen looked up quickly. "Now, wait a minute," he said. "I—"

Meg turned her back on him and walked away. "Come on, Kerry," she said, fixing Paris under her arm. "We have to start back now."

As Meg and Kerry went down the stairs, they could hear Stephen calling after them. "Hey! Wait a minute, will you?" he shouted.

The girls didn't stop.

9
THE GEORGE WASHINGTON DOLLS

Lucy folded her napkin and put it beside her plate. "What happened today?" she asked.

Across the dinner table, Meg and Kerry exchanged quick glances. "Nothing much," Meg answered.

Lucy smiled. "Something exciting happened at my office," she said. "An old, old book that we've all been waiting to see came in the morning mail. It's a diary of some kind. Workmen found it in an old barn that was being torn down. We hope to find some bits of history written down there, just as they happened. Some very important facts have been discovered that way."

Meg nodded. "Uncle Hal always tells me that," she said. "He says sometimes you don't even recognize the information at first, but you keep digging it out."

"Right," Lucy said. "That's why I'm so anxious to

read this old diary. I brought the book home, along with a bunch of magazines. I planned to read it tonight. But instead," Lucy said with a sigh, "I find I'm needed at the craft shop. And I don't like leaving you alone like this."

"Now, Lucy," Meg said.

Lucy laughed. "All right, Meg. I won't worry," she said meekly. "I'm going."

After Lucy had left, Kerry sat down at the living room desk to write a letter to her family. Meg settled down on the sofa to sew a loose button on Paris's dress—and to think. Her father always told her to figure things out for herself.

Meg kept her eyes on her sewing while her brain whirled around in circles. *There has to be a reason why Stephen wants Miss Mariah's old toys,* she told herself. *What is it? The toys aren't valuable. Miss Mariah values them because they are part of her childhood with the Colonel.*

Meg smiled as she remembered the family nickname for Ben Higgins. All of a sudden something clicked inside her head. Meg's eyes sparkled as she ran over to the desk.

"Kerry," she said, "the Colonel's little wooden dolls *were* valuable! That's why he hid them. And nobody has ever found them. Remember?"

"Of course I do," Kerry said. "What about it?"

"Listen." Meg was growing excited, but she made

herself speak slowly. "I think Stephen is here looking for those two clothespin dolls," she said.

Kerry shook her head. "No, Meg," she said. "That couldn't be right. Nobody knows about the two wooden dolls. That's Miss Mariah's secret. She never told anyone about it—until she told us. How could Stephen know about them?"

Meg frowned. "I don't know how," she admitted, "but he's found out about those dolls. And whoever is with him knows about them, too. They came here to steal the Colonel's two wooden dolls."

The idea made Kerry feel weak in her knees. "Maybe you're right, Meg," she said. "We have to be very careful. We don't even know where they are, but we can't let Stephen or anyone else find Miss Mariah's clothespin dolls."

For a minute both girls looked at each other. Then Meg managed a small smile. "Finish your letter," she said. "I'll go back to my thinking."

Restless, Meg walked over to a window and looked out at the quiet street. She tried to think, but her mind was a blank. Meg sighed and went back to her place on the sofa. As she sat down, she saw the pile of magazines that Lucy had left on the coffee table. An old book lay on top of them.

That must be the old diary Lucy was telling us about, Meg thought. She picked up the book and opened it with great care.

90

The pages were brittle and yellowed with age. Fine, old-fashioned script, full of curlicues, covered page after page. The writing was faded and difficult to read. Meg laid the book carefully on her knees and bent over it. Turning the pages with gentle hands, she wondered about the person who had written the diary such a long time ago.

In the middle of the book, Meg found an old tintype photograph. The tin plate had been mounted on a piece of cardboard, and the picture was very clear. It showed two men, looking serious and as stiff as pokers, standing beside a table. Meg studied the picture for a long time. *Which one of you kept this diary?* she wondered.

Turning the picture over, she found a few lines of plain, neat lettering on the back. Meg read the words quickly: "Taken on this eleventh day of June, in the year 1879, to mark the occasion of the sale of the George Washington dolls."

The George Washington dolls? Meg thought, frowning. *What are they? Maybe there's something more about them in the diary.* She bent over the open pages of the book.

But the old-fashioned handwriting, full of swirling lines and fancy curls, was too much for Meg. She couldn't decipher it, though she could make out a few words here and there. She was pretty sure of *George Washington,* and *River House plan,* and something about a *little girl, Martha,* or something like that. Another word that appeared several times looked like either *Colonel* or *Colonial.* That was all she could read.

Meg was discouraged. She put the old book back on the table and picked up one of the magazines. It was a copy of *Museum Notes.*

Uncle Hal always reads this, she thought as she flipped the pages. Suddenly one page caught Meg's attention. "THE MYSTERY OF THE MISSING GEORGE WASHINGTON DOLLS," the big black letters screamed at her. Meg's heart began to pound. "Kerry, come over here," she said. "Listen to this."

She read aloud, " 'The first President of the United States, George Washington, was born in Virginia in 1732.' "

Kerry sat down beside her on the sofa. Heads close together, they went on reading.

The article told about two little dolls that George Washington had made for his sister Betty. They were clothespin dolls, a very popular type of doll at that time—and George had named them Charity and Mercy.

Later, when Betty was a grown woman, she had given the dolls to a girl named Nell Benson. It was known that the Bensons had kept the dolls in the family, handing them down from generation to generation. Sam Benson was the last member of the

family known to have had them. Both clothespin dolls had suddenly disappeared, and no trace of them had ever been found.

Meg and Kerry stopped reading and looked at each other, their eyes full of wonder.

"Miss Mariah's lost dolls are clothespin dolls," Meg said excitedly.

Kerry's little nose twitched. "And they were named Mercy and Charity," she said. "Do you think—"

"I don't know," Meg said. Breathless, she turned the page, and they went on reading.

The rest of the article told about an old diary that had been found. Although the diary was unsigned, there was strong reason to believe that the book had been kept by Sam Benson. In one part of the diary, the writer told of selling the George Washington dolls to his friend, the Colonel, who had taken the dolls home to his River House plantation to give to his little girl, Mariah.

"These facts, found in the old diary, have brought new hope that the dolls made by our first President may be found someday," the article ended.

"The Colonel—River House—little girl, Mariah—" Meg's eyes were enormous. Kerry's mouth was wide open in a speechless O.

"Oh, Kerry," Meg said, "I think we've found the secret of Miss Mariah's lost dolls!"

Meg's eyes were as bright as twin stars. She lifted the old book from the coffee table.

"This is Sam Benson's diary," she cried. "I couldn't read much of the old-fashioned writing, but I did pick out the most important words."

Quickly but carefully, Meg opened the old book and found the key words again. "Write this down, Kerry," she said. "Make a list: George Washington . . . River House plan . . . little girl, Martha . . . Colonel, or Colonial."

Kerry listed the words as Meg called them. Then she handed the paper to Meg. It took only a minute for Meg to add and change a few things. When she finished, the list looked like this:

George Washington
River House ~~plan~~ plantation
little girl, ~~Martha~~ Mariah
Colonel, ~~or Colonial~~

"The Colonel simply has to be Miss Mariah's grandfather, Ben Higgins!" Meg said, very excited.

She took the old tintype from the book and handed it to Kerry. "One of these men is Sam Benson, and the other one is the Colonel," she said.

Kerry was just as excited as Meg. "Wow!" she

said. "That means Miss Mariah's clothespin dolls are the missing George Washington dolls!"

Meg beamed. "The clues are all there in that magazine article," she said. "Everything points to Miss Mariah."

Kerry nodded. "Lots of people must have read this story," she said. "I bet that's why all those strangers were going out to River House and asking questions about Miss Mariah's family and old toys."

"Right," Meg agreed, serious again. "Stephen must have seen the article, too. I was right, Kerry. Stephen's here to get the dolls."

"He has to *find* the dolls first," Kerry said. "Nobody knows where they are—not even Miss Mariah. She can only remember part of her grandfather's directions."

Meg was thoughtful. "That's right, Kerry," she said, frowning. "But why does Miss Mariah remember just that one part of the Colonel's message? She's forgotten the rest, but she remembers that part. It must be the most important part of her grandfather's directions."

"Maybe," Kerry said. "But the message doesn't really say much. It just says to keep looking and she'll find them. And Miss Mariah's looked all over the house."

Meg's frown grew deeper. "There's another thing I don't understand. What made Miss Mariah begin

The George Washington Dolls

her search in the secret room? There're lots of rooms in River House. Why did she look in the secret room first? And why was she so disappointed when the dolls weren't there?"

Meg stopped talking to think for a minute. "Kerry," she said finally, "way back in Miss Mariah's brain, maybe she remembers the Colonel telling her to look in the secret room."

"She did look there, Meg," Kerry said, a bit impatiently. "But the dolls weren't there."

Something clicked in Meg's head again, and she caught her breath. "I think I know why," she said quickly. "Miss Mariah looked in the wrong house! I think her grandfather was telling her to look in the secret room in the dollhouse!"

"Then we're out of luck for sure," Kerry said after a minute. "Stephen has searched the dollhouse. He must have the dolls!"

"Stephen didn't find them," Meg said quickly. "If he had, he wouldn't still be here in Williamsburg. He'd be gone." Meg's eyes danced. "Tomorrow morning, we'll get down to work early," she said, already making plans. "We'll open that little trapdoor in the playroom wall—and we'll find the clothespin dolls!"

It took Meg a long time to get to sleep that night. The idea of searching the dollhouse excited her, and she could hardly wait for morning. But something was bothering her—something she needed to remember. It kept teasing at the edge of her mind, but each time she almost had it, the clue slipped away again.

She was still trying to catch it when she fell asleep.

Early next morning, Meg and Kerry slipped up the back stairs to the Child's Room. They pulled the dollhouse into the middle of the floor and lifted out all the furniture. Excited, both girls looked in at the tiny trapdoor in the playroom wall.

"Hurry, Meg," Kerry urged. "Open the trapdoor."

Meg held her breath and put one hand in through the window, reaching for the tiny door. A second later she frowned.

"Oh, Kerry, I can't open it," she said. "The door has to be pulled up from the bottom, and somebody took the knob off the door! There's nothing to hold on to."

Kerry groaned. "Keep trying, Meg," she urged. "Maybe you'll be able to get it open."

Meg tried again, but she couldn't budge the little door. It remained closed, wedged tightly against the floor.

"It's no use," she sighed. "That door is stuck fast."

Kerry groaned louder. "We have to get it open," she insisted. "It's the only way we can get into the secret room under the roof and find the dolls!"

Meg was busy putting the furniture back into the rooms. "Look, Kerry," she said, "we'd have to turn the house upside down to make that trapdoor come open, and—"

Meg stopped in midsentence, her eyes widening as she repeated her words to herself. There it was—the clue she couldn't catch last night. This time she had it!

"Kerry," she cried, "that's it! We're supposed to turn the house upside down and make the trapdoor fall open!"

Kerry blinked. "Are you sure?" she asked.

Meg became very serious. "Miss Mariah didn't remember where her grandfather told her he had hidden the toys," she said. "But she has known all along how to find the dolls. She remembered that part of the Colonel's directions. She just didn't dig deep enough to get the message, that's all."

Kerry's eyes shone with excitement as she began to see what Meg was driving at.

Meg was getting pretty excited, too. "The Colonel said, 'It won't be easy, Mariah, but you'll find them. Turn the house upside down, and you'll find them.' That's exactly what she was supposed to do. Then the trapdoor would drop open, and Miss Mariah would be able to reach inside the secret room and find the dolls!"

Kerry took hold of one side of the dollhouse. "Let's

do it right now, Meg,'' she said.

''No more time,'' Meg sighed as the bell rang, signaling the start of visiting hours. ''We'll have to wait till lunch hour.''

The minute the visitors left at noontime, Meg and Kerry started to clear the dollhouse rooms again. Then, slowly, carefully, they turned the little house upside down.

The house was heavy and clumsy to handle. The big chimneys kept it from resting flat on the floor, and it wobbled and rocked in their hands.

''The Colonel was right,'' Kerry puffed, holding the house tightly. ''It sure wasn't easy to turn the house upside down.''

Meg grinned. ''You hold it steady,'' she said. ''I'll look inside.''

The first thing Meg saw was the tiny trapdoor. With the house standing upside down, the door was no longer wedged tightly against the floor. It swung a little each time the house moved.

Meg's hand shook as she reached inside the tiny playroom. She slid her hand through the narrow opening and felt all around the secret room. ''There's nothing here,'' she said finally.

''Oh, no,'' Kerry sighed.

Deeply disappointed, Meg ran her fingers over the floor, then along the walls and the roof.

"Be careful," Kerry cried. "You're pushing the roof crooked."

Meg jerked her hand back quickly. The roof settled back in place. "Ouch! There's something sharp in there," Meg said. "I hurt myself."

Pulling her hand free, Meg looked at her finger. It was only a broken fingernail. But a scrap of gray cloth dangled from her ragged nail. Meg and Kerry knew at once what it must be.

"Miss Mariah said Mercy was dressed in gray," Meg said. "This must be a piece of cloth from her dress. Mercy *was* hidden in the secret room!"

Kerry looked as if she would weep. "Oh, Meg!" she said. "Stephen did find the George Washington dolls, after all!"

10
PARIS'S SECRET

Meg didn't say a word as she and Kerry turned the dollhouse upright. She was thinking.

"No, Kerry," she said at last. "I'm almost positive that Stephen didn't find the dolls. He never heard about the upside down clue. So he wouldn't have any idea how to get into the secret room."

"Maybe you're right," Kerry said slowly.

Meg seemed puzzled as she thought of something else. "I don't think both clothespin dolls were hidden in the secret room, Kerry," she said. "That room is awfully small. There was barely enough room for one doll to fit in there. Mercy must have been squashed up under the roof all this time."

Kerry was completely confused. "Well, if Stephen doesn't have Mercy, and she's not in the dollhouse, where is she?" she asked.

"I don't know," Meg said. "But I should—and so

should you, Kerry. There's something we should both remember. I just can't think what it is."

Meg set her chin firmly. "One thing is sure: We have to find Miss Mariah's dolls before Stephen finds them," she said. "He won't leave this town until he gets them. He'll be back, Kerry."

The toy show was very crowded all afternoon. Meg and Kerry gave their talks over and over. Kerry was kept so busy that she almost forgot about missing lunch. Meg made innumerable trips into the big bedroom, showing Paris to the small children.

Late in the afternoon, Meg was walking through the crowds again. As she passed the hall door, she saw Stephen in the upstairs hallway. He was standing beside a tall man whom Meg had never seen before, and they were talking with Mr. Adam.

Seeing the three men together increased Meg's nervousness. She tightened her arms around Paris and hurried back to the Child's Room. Kerry had finished her talk, and the people were leaving.

"Stephen's here," Meg said softly. "He's with Mr. Adam and another man."

Kerry grabbed Meg's arm. "Mr. Adam?" she asked. "Where are they? Out in the hall?"

Meg nodded. Silently the girls walked through the big bedroom and looked out into the hallway. Meg wrapped her arms around Paris and huddled behind the doorframe. Kerry was right beside her.

They could see the three men over in a corner. Mr. Adam was talking. Stephen and the tall stranger listened politely.

"Well, Professor," Mr. Adam was saying in his clipped manner, "It's been nice talking with you. Now I'm afraid I must run."

The tall man smiled slightly and nodded. "Of course," he said. "Stephen and I won't keep you."

Mr. Adam smiled in return; then, with a slight bow of his head, he went down the stairs.

Stephen turned to the tall man. The man's handsome face was grave. "It's time we tend to our business, Stephen. We don't have much time left. We leave here in the morning. Now, get hold of Meg and Kerry and bring them to me! I must talk with those two girls!"

"Okay," Stephen said. "You're the boss." He looked serious as he followed the tall man down the wide stairs. "I'll come back here today and see what I can do."

"Meg," Kerry gasped after a long moment. "Stephen's stopped. I think he's coming back!" As she spoke, she clutched Meg's arm, jerking her sharply and throwing her off-balance. Meg tried to keep a tight hold on Paris, but she lost her grip, and the little doll began to fall.

Frantically Meg made a grab for the doll. There was no time to be gentle. Meg's only thought was

104

to save Paris from smashing to pieces on the floor. In the nick of time, her fingers caught an edge of soft silk. Paris dangled mere inches above the floor.

"Is—is she all right?" Kerry asked, almost afraid to look.

Very gingerly, Meg examined the doll. "I guess so," she said slowly. "Wait! There's a funny big lump on Paris's back!"

With timid fingers, Meg touched it. The strange lump moved! There was a loud *pop,* as if something had burst open. Paris flopped over in Meg's arms, and there was a thin, tinny wail: "Mama."

"That was Paris!" Meg said, amazed.

"Paris is talking!" Kerry gasped.

Meg's quick eyes had seen something. A tiny scrap of black cloth was showing at the back of Paris's neck. Meg covered it with her hands and traced her fingers down over the lump. Was it—could it be— Suddenly the words the Colonel had spoken to Miss Mariah so many years ago echoed in Meg's ears: *"She can't talk now, but maybe someday she will."*

Feeling the lump under her fingers, Meg knew she had found Paris's secret!

"Kerry," she said, "we have to find Lucy right away. Stephen will be coming back, and we can't be here when he comes. I'm certain that he and the Professor plan to get the George Washington dolls tonight!"

Kerry turned pale. "What will we do?"

Meg managed to keep her voice calm. "Run downstairs and tell the senior hostess that we have to leave right away," she said. "Lucy said something about working at the old jail today. Maybe we can find her there."

While Kerry was downstairs, Meg took the sash from her dress and put it around Paris. She wrapped it as tightly as she could and hoped that the wide sash would hold. Her hands were shaking.

If only Constable Hosey were here, Meg thought as she tied the sash into a knot. Constable Hosey was in charge of police affairs back in Hidden Springs. He had helped Meg and Kerry before, several times, when they were working on a mystery.

This time he couldn't, so Meg's only thought was to get to Lucy. And she had to keep Paris's secret until she found Lucy!

11
THE
PROFESSOR

The Public Gaol was quite a distance from Brush-Everard House. Meg and Kerry ran all the way. They were hot and breathless when they rushed into the keeper's quarters at the old jail. The keeper was busy at his desk.

"Sorry," he said, without raising his head, "visiting hours are over. Come back tomorrow."

Meg tightened her arms around Paris. "We're looking for Miss Lucy Cameron," she told him. "We thought we could find her here."

The keeper looked up and smiled. "You must be the two little ladies from the toy show," he said. He scratched his head and thought for a moment. "I don't remember seeing Miss Lucy, but that doesn't mean she isn't here. Go on in and look, but be quick about it. I'm about ready to close up."

Meg and Kerry hurried along the narrow, empty

hallway. The gloomy old prison made them nervous.

They crossed the dismal yard, where prisoners used to walk, and entered the main part of the old jail. The doors to the cells yawned open, showing dirt floors and straw sleeping mats. Thin slivers of light entered through the small, high windows.

Without a word, Meg and Kerry proceeded along the dim corridor. They saw no sign of Lucy. Finally they stopped in front of the open door of the last cell.

"This is the solitary confinement cell," Meg said in an awed tone. "Maybe this is the very place where Bluebeard's pirates were held."

Kerry shivered as she peered into the cell.

Something about the lonely place drew them like a magnet. They stepped inside.

The air was heavy with the smell of dampness. There was no sleeping mat, no window. The stub of a candle flickered on the wall at the far end of the room.

"Come on, Meg," Kerry said, her voice quivering. "Let's go."

Meg didn't need to be coaxed. She stepped out into the hall—then ducked back in. "A man is coming down the corridor," she whispered. "Stand way back so he won't see us if he looks in here."

Meg and Kerry quietly made their way to the darkest corner of the cell. There was a sudden loud

bang, then the sharp click of a key turning in a lock. The candle flame jumped, sputtered, and almost went out.

"Kerry!" Meg cried. "Somebody just locked the door. We're locked in!"

Shaking with fright, they groped their way back to the door.

"Help! Help!" Meg shouted.

"Let us out of here!" Kerry yelled.

Pounding and kicking the door, they continued to shout for help. Once they thought they heard someone in the corridor. They yelled until their throats were sore, but no one came. Finally they had to stop and rest.

The flickering light of the candle cast eerie shadows on the bare stone walls of the cell. As Meg watched, the shadows began to fade into almost total darkness. The glow from the candle dimmed and dipped to almost nothing. Meg knew that the candle wouldn't last much longer. The thought of spending the night locked in the cell frightened her.

"Let's try again, Kerry," she said. "When I count up to three, we'll both shout together. One . . . two . . . three!"

"Help! Help!" they shouted. "Open the door!"

A few seconds later they heard voices out in the hall. "I can't understand how anything like this could happen," a man's voice was saying. "Surely

110

you must check inside each cell before you lock the door."

"Now, look, mister," a grumpy voice replied, "I'm not a guide around here. I'm the night watchman. It's my duty to lock things up. Nobody's supposed to be in here when I come to work. And there's nobody down here now, like I told you."

"I know the two girls came in here," the first man insisted, "and they didn't come out again. Unlock the cell doors, please."

Meg didn't need to wait any longer. "We're down here in the last cell," she shouted.

There was the sound of a heavy key being turned in the lock. Pushing the door open, Meg and Kerry rushed out into the corridor. They found themselves facing Stephen and the tall man Mr. Adam had called "Professor."

Meg's eyes widened. She tried to hide Paris in the folds of her skirt. No matter what happened, she couldn't let this man take Miss Mariah's doll.

"It's the Professor," Kerry said in a shaky voice.

The tall man smiled as he stepped closer. "Please don't be afraid," he said. "Believe me, I am your friend. You must trust me. I'm Professor Anderson, Stephen's father."

Meg and Kerry looked at each other, amazed.

"You're Stephen's father?" Meg asked.

"Right." Stephen grinned. "Dad to me, Professor

to you and to his students. And Son—''

The Professor held up his hand. "That's enough, Stephen," he said.

"Look, mister," the watchman cut in, "it doesn't matter to me what people call you. If you want to talk, go outside and talk. This place is closed for the night, so move along."

The Professor laughed good-naturedly. "I see there's no time to explain things now," he said as the watchman hurried them all to the exit. "We'll talk on the way. I've been in touch with Miss Cameron, and she thinks it best that I bring both of you along to her house. We'll have to walk around the corner to my car."

"Only the tour bus is allowed on this street," Stephen added.

Meg and Kerry had nothing to say. They followed Stephen and his father across the dark prison yard and out to the sidewalk.

"I don't trust them, Meg," Kerry whispered.

"Shhh . . . they'll hear you," Meg warned. Her dark eyes were troubled. Questions throbbed inside her head. Who was Professor Anderson? Had Lucy really asked him to bring the girls home? Should they trust this man?

Meg tightened her arms around Paris and felt the strange lump on the little doll's back. She couldn't take a chance! She watched a tour bus turn the corner and start down the street. Right at that moment, Meg knew what to do.

"Kerry," she whispered softly, close to Kerry's ear, "we can't take any chances. We have to take care of Paris."

Stephen's voice interrupted her. "Are you coming?" he called back over his shoulder.

"We're right behind you," Meg answered.

Lowering her voice, Meg said to Kerry, "Slow down as much as you can without being noticed. When the bus gets close, I'll signal it to stop. When it does, climb on fast."

A few moments later they were inside the bus.

Kerry still looked worried. "How are we going to get back to Lucy's?" she asked. "The tour bus doesn't go near her street."

Meg had a plan all ready. "We'll use the shortcut through the backyard gardens," she explained. "Stephen and his father will probably use their car to search for us, and they won't be able to see us."

The bus was moving down the Duke of Gloucester Street now. They were almost up to Market Square. Meg and Kerry stepped off when the bus stopped at the square.

The dark street was completely deserted as the tour bus drove away. Quickly they darted across the street and raced over the green, past the old guardhouse, past the magazine. Kerry had her hand on

113

the first garden gate when they heard the footsteps behind them.

"Stop! Stop, you two!" a man shouted. "I'm tired of playing games. I want that doll!"

"Hurry, Meg!" Kerry cried.

Meg looked back quickly over her shoulder. She couldn't make out the man's face in the darkness, but she was sure she had recognized the voice. "Kerry!" she shouted. "It's not the Professor! It's Mr. Adam!"

12
DISCOVERY
IN THE
WOODSHED

"Mr. Adam?" Kerry yelled, surprised.

Meg gave her a push as Kerry hesitated. "Keep going," she cried. "He's right behind us!"

The two girls streaked through the dark garden. They could hear the man behind them, crashing his way through the flower beds.

"He's getting closer!" Meg shouted.

Kerry yanked Meg into the next garden and slammed the gate hard, snapping the lock in place. "That'll slow him down," she said.

A second later they heard a dull thud, followed immediately by a yelp of pain. "You girls may as well give up," the man shouted. "I won't allow you to steal a fortune from under my nose."

Meg and Kerry were way ahead of him now. Two more gardens to cross and they would be home. They could see the big chimney on Lucy's house looming ahead of them in the darkness.

Suddenly Meg gasped. The sash binding Paris was coming loose!

Meg didn't dare stop, for fear their pursuer would catch up to them. Her hands were shaking as she tightened her fingers over the lump on Paris's back.

"Kerry," she called as they both raced into Lucy's backyard, "you'll have to open the chimney door. I have to hold Paris!"

Kerry was already holding the door open. "Get in," she cried.

The next minute Meg and Kerry were inside the old woodshed, the hidden door closed behind them.

"We're safe now," Meg said breathlessly.

"Are you sure that was Mr. Adam?" Kerry asked. "I still can't believe it!"

Meg's heart was still hammering like thunder in her ears. "I'm certain of it, Kerry. He's after the George Washington dolls. He must be working with Stephen and his father. They tried to get us first. Then, when we got away from them, they must have told Mr. Adam. He was probably waiting in the car."

"But why do they want Paris?" Kerry wondered aloud.

In the darkness, Meg felt for the lump on Paris's back. The lump had grown bigger, and there was a wide tear down the back of the doll's dress.

116

Meg reached for Kerry's hand. "I have some-thng to tell you," she said. "We'd better get into the living room. Mr. Adam might find the hidden door."

They inched their way across the dark woodshed. They were almost to the living room door when they heard something roll along the floor.

"My foot just hit something," Kerry said. "Did you drop anything?"

Meg's hand flew to Paris's back. The lump was gone! Paris flipped over in her arms, and a thin, tinny "Mama" wailed through the dark shed.

"Meg!" Kerry, startled, stopped dead. "Paris just spoke *again!*"

"And I know why," Meg told her.

Opening the living room door, Meg snapped on a lamp. Only a narrow beam of light reached into the woodshed. The old shed was still quite dark.

"Now, listen, Kerry," Meg said excitedly. *"I just dropped a George Washington doll!"*

Kerry clapped her hands to her mouth. "A George Washington doll!" she sputtered. "But how—"

Meg was down on her knees in the middle of the shed, her hands searching the floor. "Don't talk— just look," she said. "I'll tell you all about it when we find the doll."

Kerry knelt down close to the wall and began to feel carefully along the dirt floor.

Meg looked up just as Kerry squealed.

"I've got it!" they both cried out at the very same moment.

Meg looked at Kerry. Kerry looked at Meg. Then both girls crawled toward the light from the door, to get a better look at what they had found.

Each girl held out one hand, then gasped aloud. Each of them was holding a tiny old-fashioned clothespin doll. Puzzled, Meg stared at the little doll in Kerry's hand. Kerry's eyes were almost popping out of her head as she, in turn, stared at the doll that Meg was holding.

Too surprised to speak, Meg and Kerry turned the dolls over and saw the initials cut into the wooden heads. " 'BW . . . GW, 1742,' " they read together in one voice.

"To Betty Washington from George Washington —made in 1742," Meg said slowly. "Over two hundred years ago!"

Kerry's eyes were enormous. "No wonder the Colonel's dolls are so valuable," she said. "They were made by our first President!" She sighed happily. "How did you ever find them, Meg?" she asked. "Where were they? How come you dropped the two dolls—"

"Wait a minute, Kerry," Meg broke in. "I didn't drop two dolls. I dropped only this one."

Meg held out the doll she had picked up from the

woodshed floor. The doll was small, and it was easy to see she had been made from a clothespin. Her face was almost cross, with a stern red mouth and two round dot eyes painted on the knob. Her painted black hair had a wide white part down the middle of her wooden knob head, and she wore a black dress and a blue shawl.

"That's Charity," Kerry said. "Where did you find her?"

Meg smiled. "Hidden inside Paris," she said. "The seam down Paris's back just split wide open, and Charity fell out on the floor."

Kerry's nose began its wiggle of excitement. "Meg," she said, "I bet the Colonel put both dolls in the same place! Mercy must have been right there beside Charity, hidden inside Paris. You must have dropped both clothespin dolls."

"No, Kerry." Meg shook her head. "Mercy was hidden inside the secret room in Miss Mariah's doll-house. We know that, because we found a piece of her dress there."

Meg took the little doll from Kerry's hand and held her carefully. The doll had a funny little face —two round dot eyes and a smiling red mouth. Her hair was as yellow as corn on the cob. She wore a long gray dress, with a plain white shawl folded around her stiff wooden shoulders. A tiny piece of cloth was missing from her skirt.

119

Very carefully Meg took the scrap of gray cloth from her pocket and held it against the tear in Mercy's dress. It matched perfectly.

"That proves it," she said. "Mercy was hidden in the dollhouse."

Kerry looked confused. "But if Mercy was hidden in the dollhouse, how did she get here—in Lucy's woodshed?" she asked.

Meg's dark eyes were big and shiny. "You and I left her here—when we dropped the dollhouse," she said.

Kerry's mouth dropped open with amazement. "We did?" she cried.

Meg giggled softly. "It took me a long time to figure things out," she said, "but I think this is the way it happened."

Her voice quickened with excitement. "I remembered that Miss Mariah told us her two little cousins had broken Paris's arms and legs," she said. "But she hadn't said anything about Paris's kid body being pulled apart. So I kept wondering why the Colonel had put that messy-looking thick seam down the doll's back."

Meg tucked a piece of cotton stuffing inside the doll's split seam before she went on. "I think the Colonel must have hidden Charity inside Paris to make sure his valuable doll would be safe. That's why Paris was so lumpy—and it's also why she couldn't speak. Charity was pressed up tight against her voice box. The Colonel couldn't sew very well, of course, and he knew his poor sewing would let go someday, and Paris would begin to talk. And then Charity would be found.''

Kerry nodded. "I guess that's why he told Miss Mariah to listen to Paris," she said.

Meg looked at the happy-faced doll. "I think the Colonel found Mercy inside the secret room in the dollhouse," she went on. "But he couldn't get her out, because his hand was too big. So when he tried to pull Mercy free, he only pushed her in tighter, and Mercy got wedged up under the dollhouse roof. That's why the roof was crooked.

"The Colonel couldn't get her free, so he had to leave her there. He took the doorknob off the trapdoor in the dollhouse playroom so that no one could reach inside the secret room. The only way to get the trapdoor open was to tip the dollhouse upside down."

Kerry nodded. "And then he told Miss Mariah exactly how to find the doll," she said. "But she was so sick, she didn't remember everything her grandfather told her to do."

Meg was thoughtful for a long minute. "You know, Kerry," she said at last, "we were pretty lucky when we dropped the dollhouse that day. The house landed right side up, but that jarred the roof just hard enough to make it pop up, and Mercy was thrown out on the floor. If the house had landed upside down, Mercy might have fallen back farther inside the dollhouse. Then Stephen would have found her when he searched the house.''

Kerry caught her breath. "That's right, Meg," she said. "And you know something else? I bet it was Mercy that Lucy tripped over that night when—"

"Shh," Meg said. "Someone's coming!"

Meg and Kerry slipped the little dolls into their pockets and moved back against the wall. In their excitement, they had forgotten that they might still be in danger. Was it Mr. Adam who had come in that unlocked front door? They could hear someone walking in the living room now.

"Hey there," Lucy's voice called out. "Meg! Kerry! Are you home?"

"Where are you, Maggie-me-love?" Hal Ashley shouted.

13

THE PROFESSOR'S STORY

"Uncle Hal!" Meg shouted.

The next minute, Meg was squeezing her uncle in a tight bear hug.

"What were you two kids doing out in the woodshed?" he asked, hugging both girls at once.

Meg and Kerry exchanged secretive looks, then Meg's eyes sparkled. "Did you ever hear about the lost George Washington dolls?" she asked.

Her uncle's face turned serious. "That was a well-kept secret, Meg," he said. "What do you know about the lost George Washington dolls?"

"We found them!" Meg exclaimed delightedly as she and Kerry handed him the two wooden dolls.

Quickly Hal Ashley turned the little dolls over and found the initials. "These really are the George Washington dolls," he said incredulously. "Where did you find them, Maggie?"

"One of them was right here in Lucy's woodshed, Mr. Ashley," Kerry told him.

Hal Ashley shook his head, hardly able to believe his eyes. "Come on out here and tell us the whole story," he said, walking farther into the big room. Meg and Kerry followed him. Stepping around a corner of the room, they saw the Professor sitting there, with Stephen standing beside him.

"Oh, no!" Meg cried out. Kerry went pale.

Uncle Hal saw at once that something was wrong. "What's the matter?" he asked.

The Professor wiggled in his chair. He looked most uncomfortable. "I'm afraid it's my fault," he said. "Meg and Kerry are afraid of me, for some reason I can't understand."

Standing up, the man walked over to the girls. "I'm going to tell you a story," he said. "Perhaps then we'll be friends."

Meg sat close to Uncle Hal, her eyes glued to the Professor. Kerry stared at the man suspiciously.

"Well," the Professor began, "a good number of years ago, an elderly gentleman here in Williamsburg had a birthday party. He was eighty-five years old."

Meg and Kerry looked at each other. "Just like Miss Mariah's grandfather," Meg whispered.

"The party was held at his River House plantation," the Professor went on. His voice low with memories, he told the same story that Meg and Kerry

had heard at River House on Saturday afternoon.

Meg's mouth was wide open with amazement. "That's the same story Miss Mariah Collins told us about her grandfather's birthday party," she said when the Professor had finished. "How do you know it?"

The man's smile was almost sad. "I was there, at the Colonel's party, Meg," he answered. "I was the boy who hid the two wooden dolls."

"Are you Sonny?" Kerry gasped.

"I am," the Professor admitted.

Meg leaned forward eagerly, all her fear of this man gone. "Where did you hide the dolls, Professor?" she asked. "Do you remember?"

"Yes, I remember that very well," the Professor said. "I hid them both in the dollhouse. I had found a small room behind a trapdoor."

"The secret room," Meg said softly.

"I put the doll with the happy face and the yellow hair inside that small room. There wasn't much space, but I managed to push her inside. There was no room left for the little black-haired doll, though. So I dropped her behind the toy sofa in the dollhouse living room."

"But why didn't you tell someone where you had put the dolls?" Kerry asked.

Professor Anderson smiled broadly. "For the very good reason that nobody asked me. Cousin Mariah and my mother, Florabelle, have never spoken to each other since that day. And Jane and I were forbidden to mention the Colonel's party.''

Uncle Hal was as anxious as Meg and Kerry to hear all the details. "Tell me, Professor," he asked, "when did you find out about the lost George Washington dolls?"

The man looked uncomfortable again. "You may find this hard to believe, Mr. Ashley," he said. "It was exactly two weeks ago—and it was quite by accident that I read the article about the dolls in *Museum Notes* magazine."

The Professor shook his head, remembering his discovery. "As soon as I had read it, I knew I was responsible for the disappearance of the two George Washington dolls," he sighed. "Of course, all the family knew about Cousin Mariah's locked room, and I had an idea it might be the old playroom. I thought it was just possible that the dolls might still be there in the dollhouse. I felt duty-bound to tell Cousin Mariah about this."

Stephen spoke up for the first time. "Dad knew Cousin Mariah would never see him, because of that crazy family feud business," he said. "So we both came to Williamsburg, and Dad sent me out to River House." Stephen grinned and shrugged his shoulders. "It didn't do much good," he said. "Cousin Mariah wouldn't even let me in."

Everybody laughed.

"Now I know how you knew all about Miss Mariah and her toys," Meg said with a chuckle. "Your father told you."

"Right," Stephen said. "And as soon as I told Dad about the crooked roof on the dollhouse, he guessed right away that the roof was being pushed out of line by the doll."

The Professor looked serious. "When Stephen told me that the roof was perfectly straight after you people dropped the dollhouse in the woodshed, I thought it very likely that the bump had dislodged the doll. But I couldn't say whether the doll had bounced back inside the house or outside, onto the woodshed floor," he said.

"Mercy landed outside, Professor," Meg explained. "That's where we just found her."

"We were awfully surprised, too," Kerry put in. "We had no idea she was there."

"We tried to tell you," Stephen said quickly. "Dad sent me around to the toy show to see if the clothespin doll had fallen back inside the dollhouse. But there didn't seem to be a sign of a wooden doll there. So then Dad and I were sure the doll was here, in the woodshed. I phoned you that night, but you wouldn't let us come over."

Meg looked embarrassed. "I'm sorry about that, Stephen," she said. "Kerry and I were sure you were trying to steal Miss Mariah's old toys.''

"Steal them!" Stephen yelped. "My gosh! I was trying to help you find them!''

Kerry spoke up in self-defense. "Well, you stole Paris,'' she said. "We know it was you, because we saw the mud on your shoes. And it was the same kind as the footprints on the back stairs.''

Stephen grinned. "I didn't *steal* Paris,'' he said. "I saw the doll on the counter, and I thought you had forgotten her. So I picked her up and brought her to Brush-Everard House. When I was coming up the back stairway, I heard Miss Cameron saying something about calling the police. So I left—fast.''

Meg looked at him and frowned. "Why did you search the dollhouse?'' she asked.

"Now, wait a minute,'' Stephen said quickly. "I checked to see if the doll had fallen back inside, but I wouldn't exactly call that a search!''

Meg looked him right in the eye. "We found your cuff link,'' she said.

Stephen shook his head. "Not my cuff link,'' he said. "I never wear them. Do I, Dad?''

"That's right,'' Professor Anderson said. "But something else is bothering me right now.'' He picked up the wooden doll with the black hair. "This little doll couldn't have been behind the dollhouse sofa all these years. Where did you find Charity?''

Meg and Kerry exchanged sly smiles.

"Charity was hidden inside Paris," Meg said. She tipped Paris forward, and once more the little doll cried, "Mama." Then she showed him the wide-open seam down Paris's back.

"Amazing!" Professor Anderson said.

Uncle Hal took Paris in his hands. "It's almost unbelievable," he said, looking at the old doll. "What a perfect hiding place. No one would ever think of looking there."

Kerry shivered slightly. "Yes, they would, Mr. Ashley," she said. "That Mr. Adam figured out Paris's secret and tried to get Paris away from us. He chased us tonight."

"But he didn't catch us, Uncle Hal," Meg broke in quickly, seeing the worried look on his face.

Hal Ashley put his arm around Meg and drew her close. "Now, start from the beginning, Maggie, and tell us all about this Mr. Adam," he said gently.

Taking turns, Meg and Kerry told about Mr. Adam, with his clipped British accent and his strange smile.

"And when we saw Stephen and the Professor talking with him today," Meg finished, "we thought they were all working together. That's why we were afraid of you, Professor. We were sure you had come here to get Miss Mariah's old dolls."

The Professor shook his head. "I'm terribly sorry, Meg," he said. "Stephen and I don't know that man.

He happened to be staying at our motel, and we talked a bit, that's all.''

Hal Ashley reached into his briefcase and pulled out a newspaper clipping. Meg saw that it was the picture she had seen in Lucy's dining room.

"Is this the man you're talking about?" he asked.

Kerry took a quick look. "No, that's not Mr. Adam," she said.

Meg studied the picture closely. There was something about the shape of the man's mouth and the small eyes staring out at her. . . . Suddenly Meg's heart skipped a beat.

"Wait a minute!" she said excitedly. She took her small sketching pad from her pocket. She flipped the pages to the picture she needed. It was a close-up front view of Mr. Adam's face. His smile was partly hidden by his full, bushy moustache. His long dark hair was neat and shiny, and his eyes looked straight out at her. Meg's hand shook with excitement. "May I try something, Uncle Hal?" she asked, taking the newspaper clipping from him.

Meg's pencil flew over the picture, adding a line, deepening a shadow, shaping and changing. When she had finished, she laid the picture beside her own drawing of Mr. Adam.

Both pictures showed the same man!

"Maggie-me-love!" Uncle Hal sounded excited. "Let me see that cuff link you found, will you?"

131

One quick look at the engraved *S* on the cuff link satisfied Hal Ashley. "Meg and Kerry," he said, very seriously, "your Mr. Adam is the man we museum people call Scott. We knew Adam Scott was around here somewhere. I was sent here to find him. Scott is one of the cleverest art thieves in the world."

Meg's eyes widened. "You mean you came here to catch a thief, Uncle Hal?" she asked.

"That's right, Maggie," Hal answered. "He's stolen treasures from under our noses before. He keeps the real treasure for himself and sells a forged copy of it. The man is an artist! He can copy any-thing—jewels, carvings, dolls—he does it all. Scott's forged treasures have fooled even the experts. The authorities have been after him for years, but some-how he always slips through their fingers."

Meg was growing excited. "You can catch him this time, Uncle Hal," she cried. "He didn't get the dolls yet. He's probably back at the motel!"

"She's right, Hal," Lucy cried.

Stephen was already at the door. "We'll show you the way, Mr. Ashley," he said.

Hal Ashley grabbed his briefcase and said, "Give me a few minutes to call the police. I'll want a policeman sent over to the motel, and then we'll all go. Meg and Kerry can identify this man as the one who chased them tonight, and I can hold him for trying to steal the George Washington dolls."

14

"LISTEN TO PARIS"

In a very short time they were all at the motel parking lot. Out of the corner of her eye, Meg saw a policeman approaching. Uncle Hal met him, and the two of them huddled together briefly, talking fast. Meg was too far away to hear what was said.

Finally Uncle Hal returned to the rest of the group and, speaking very softly, said, "Okay, Professor. Everything's ready. Let's go."

With the Professor and Stephen leading the way, everyone headed for Mr. Adam's motel unit.

Meg looked back for the police officer. "Isn't the policeman coming with us?" she asked her uncle.

"Don't worry, Meg," Hal assured her. "The policeman is not allowed to enter Mr. Adam's room or search for anything without a warrant. If we can just prove that your Mr. Adam is guilty of breaking a law, the policeman will be right here to take him away." Hal's face hardened. "And I'm pretty sure we'll do just that," he said.

The Professor had stopped in front of Mr. Adam's door. Meg saw him knock, then saw the door open. Mr. Adam stood in the doorway.

"Oh, good evening, Professor," he said in his clipped speech. "This is a surprise."

The Professor smiled. "May we come in?"

Mr. Adam looked a bit confused. "Of course, of course," he said finally. "I was getting ready to go out for a late dinner. I was, ah, detained by some business." He held the door open and waved the Professor and Stephen into the room.

Hal Ashley stepped out of the shadows. "Just a minute, Scott," he said quietly. "We have a few questions to ask you."

Meg saw the alarmed look on the man's face, but it was gone in a flash. "I beg your pardon," he said. "My name is Adam. I believe you have made a mistake."

He smiled faintly and started to close the door. Hal Ashley was too quick for him. He was inside the room before Mr. Adam knew it. Meg, Kerry, and Lucy followed him.

"No, Scott," Hal said, "*you* made the mistake, when you came to Williamsburg to look for the George Washington dolls."

Mr. Adam turned to the Professor. "George

134

Washington dolls?'' he asked. "Is this a joke of some sort?''

Hal Ashley's face hardened. "Look here, Scott, we know you came here to get the dolls,'' he said. "And you might have gotten away with your scheme if it hadn't been for two smart girls.''

Mr. Adam stared at him coldly. "I don't know what you're talking about,'' he said.

Meg couldn't keep quiet any longer. "Oh, yes, you do,'' she said. "I don't know how you found out, but you discovered Paris's secret. And you tried to take her away from us tonight.'' Turning to her uncle, Meg said, "He's the man we were telling you about, Uncle Hal.''

Kerry's dander was really up. "He's the one who chased us through the gardens, Mr. Ashley,'' she cried.

The man glared down at Meg and Kerry. "What are you two children trying to do?'' he asked.

Hal Ashley took hold of his arm. "We've been after you for a long time, Scott,'' he said.

"Take your hand off my arm,'' Mr. Adam said sharply, pulling away. "You can't hold me for anything. You have nothing on me. You can't prove one thing.''

Abruptly he turned his back and walked over to his dresser. Personal effects from his pockets were spread out on top of the dresser. "If you will excuse

135

me," he said, "I was about ready to leave for dinner."
Calmly he began to pick up his things and return
them to his pockets.

Meg's heart sank. She had a terrible feeling that
this thief was going to get away again. She had to
think of something!

With angry eyes, Meg watched Mr. Adam as he
put things into various pockets: comb, wallet, keys,
papers. . . .

Suddenly Meg spied something on the dresser.
In one quick movement, she was across the room
and had it in her hand.

"Is this your cuff link, Mr. Adam?" she asked.

There was a hint of a sneer in the man's smile. "Of
course it's my cuff link," he said. "It would hardly
be here on my dresser if it weren't. Unfortunately
I've lost the mate."

Meg took the matching cuff link from her pocket.
"Really?" she said. "Is this it?"

Eyes blazing, Kerry spoke up. "You dropped your
cuff link at the toy show," she said heatedly. "And
we found it—in the Child's Room!"

Again the man looked alarmed. "I believe the
toy show was open to the public," he said, fighting
to appear calm. "I had a perfect right to be there."

"But you had no right to search Miss Mariah's
dollhouse," Meg pressed on. "You thought the George
Washington dolls were hidden in that toy house, and

you were looking for them so you could steal them! That's where you dropped your cuff link, Mr. Adam —inside the dollhouse!''

Mr. Adam's face turned gray. His polished manners disappeared. "You two fresh, nosy little brats!" he growled. "Give me that cuff link!''

He made a quick lunge for Meg, but Hal was there, pinning his arms to his sides. "You're a clever man, Scott," he said, "but these two young detectives are a little smarter. I'm having you held on suspicion of the attempted theft of the George Washington dolls. I suspect the authorities will have no trouble finding additional charges.''

Hal led Adam Scott to the door. The policeman was standing there, waiting.

"Take care of this man," Hal said. "I'll be down to the station shortly. He's wanted for a lot of things.''

"Yes, sir,'' the policeman said. He led Adam Scott away.

It was two-thirty Saturday afternoon. Meg and Kerry watched Miss Mariah Collins close the tattered old book and lay it down beside her on the sofa. For a long moment she studied the old tintype she held in her hand. With just a trace of a smile, Mariah looked around at the people gathered in her living room.

"Just think of that,'' she sighed. "My granddaddy's

two wooden dolls were made by George Washington himself!''

Meg and Kerry smiled happily. "He really did have two valuable dolls, didn't he?" Meg said.

Mariah nodded. "Indeed he did, Meg," she said with a smile. "Sam Benson's diary makes that very clear." She glanced at the tintype again. "Granddaddy often talked about his old friend. I have a number of pictures of them together. If I may, I would like very much to add this one to my collection."

"Of course you may," Lucy said. "I think it should stay here with you."

Mariah smiled as she looked at the tall man sitting beside her on the sofa. "Sonny Anderson," she said, pretending to be cross, "you started all this. If you hadn't hidden those two little dolls— I suppose I should spank you, but I won't. I'm much too happy to have you and Stephen here with me. When will Florabelle arrive?"

Professor Anderson patted his cousin's hand. "Mother and my wife will be here in the morning," he said.

The elderly lady smiled. "It will be so nice to see Florabelle again. It's been a long time."

She slipped the tintype between the pages of the worn book and laid it on the table, beside Charity and Mercy. Miss Mariah looked at the two dolls, almost unable to believe they were there. "It's been a long time since I've seen Granddaddy's clothespin dolls," she said with a little smile.

Meg and Kerry looked at each other and grinned.

"Ask her now," Kerry whispered.

Excited, Meg sat on the edge of her chair. "Miss Mariah, were you surprised when Lucy told you where we found the dolls?" she asked.

Lucy began to laugh. "I didn't get a chance to tell her!" she said. "Miss Mariah told me! I said, 'Something wonderful has happened. Meg and Kerry turned your dollhouse upside down—' "

" 'And found Granddaddy's clothespin doll in the secret room!' I said," Miss Mariah broke in, her face beaming. "The very minute I heard Lucy say those words, I remembered where Granddaddy had told me I would find this doll."

Taking Mercy from the table, Mariah held the happy-looking doll in her hands. "Everything came back to me again. I remembered how the Colonel had told me that this little doll was stuck in the secret room and that he couldn't pull her free. He told me how he had taken the doorknob off the trapdoor, to be sure no one could get her.

" 'You'll have to tip the dollhouse upside down to make the trapdoor drop open,' he told me, 'and it won't be easy, Mariah, but you'll find her. Turn the house upside down, and you'll find her.' So, you see, I did remember his directions, after all."

139

Meg's eyes sparkled. "In a way, you were right all along, Miss Mariah," she said. "You kept thinking that Mercy was in a secret room."

"Your subconscious mind got the rooms mixed up, that's all," Kerry said.

"I guess that's about right, Kerry," said Miss Mariah. "And, as for Charity—" she looked at the black-haired doll on the table—"well, I guess Granddaddy never imagined for one moment that his poor sewing would hold together all this time. That's why he just laughed and told me to listen to Paris."

Meg sighed with contentment. "Well, anyhow, you have both clothespin dolls now," she said, "and that's the important part."

She walked across to Miss Mariah and handed Paris back to her. Mariah tipped Paris over and laughed affectionately when the old doll wailed, "Mama!"